NIGHTWALKERS

JUDY K. MORRIS

HarperCollins*Publishers*

Library of Congress Cataloging-in-Publication Data

Morris, Judy K.

    Nightwalkers / Judy K. Morris.

       p.   cm.

    Summary: After a school trip to the Washington zoo, ten-year-old James becomes so attached to Daisy, an orphaned African elephant, that he jeopardizes his placement in a new foster home to accompany her on several desperate nighttime journeys.

    ISBN 0-06-027200-7 — ISBN 0-06-027201-5 (lib. bdg.)

    [1. Elephants—Fiction. 2. Foster home care—Fiction. 3. Afro-Americans—Fiction.] I. Title.

PZ7.M8283Ni   1996   96-16241

[Fic]—dc20   CIP

                                             AC

Typography by Gail M. Hess

1 2 3 4 5 6 7 8 9 10

First Edition

For Jonas Morris
who built the table on which I work

Nature's great master-peece, an Elephant,
The onely harmlesse great thing; the giant
Of beasts; . . .
Himselfe he up-props, on himselfe relies,
And foe to none, suspects no enemies. . . .

John Donne
The Progresse of the Soule (1601)

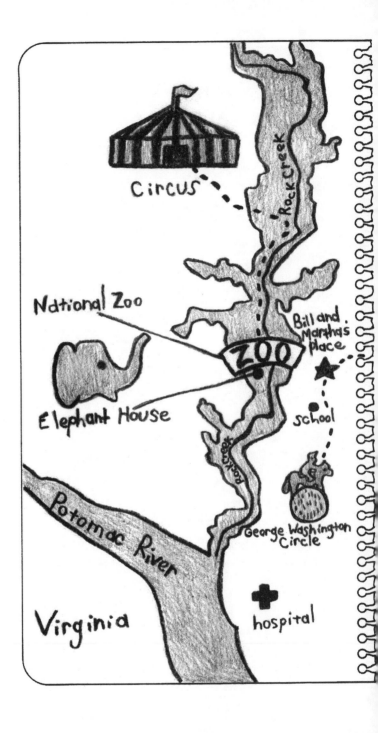

Nightwalking with Daisy around Washington, D.C.

the hunk of
concrete

Big Jim and
Mama's house

Library

White House

THE ASSIGNMENT

"James, why don't you take an elephant?" Ms. Jackson suggested. "Hmmm?"

James didn't answer. He didn't care. He moved away from some boys who were squabbling and worked his skinny body into a space by the fence between two other children. Then he looked across the bare yard.

By the big stone building, zookeepers were using a thick hose to give two elephants a bath. The powerful stream of water turned their gray-and-brown skin almost black.

"Beverly! Stand!" one keeper said. Even down on her belly, Beverly was almost as tall as her keeper. Now she lunged forward, then heaved her weight up and back. Putting one heavy leg in place at a time, Beverly rose and rose until it seemed she would never stop. James took a small step backward.

"Menika! Open!" the other keeper said. When Menika opened her mouth, the keeper aimed the water inside. After Menika had a long drink, the keeper called, "Menika! Ear!" Menika held an ear forward, and the keeper sprayed behind it.

"Good girl!" The keeper blew into the end of Menika's trunk. As she moved to Menika's other side, the trunk followed her, and she blew into it again. The trunk had pink patches on it; these elephants had more colors than James expected.

A woman with a microphone was speaking to the crowd. "Imagine a nine-thousand-pound animal obeying a human who weighs just a hundred and thirty pounds!"

The fourth graders murmured at that! A boy asked if he could do his report on an elephant.

"James is doing an elephant," Ms. Jackson said and patted James's shoulder. "You have half an hour. Take notes and write down the questions you'll want your research to answer. Okay?"

James nodded and balanced his spiral notebook on the fence rail. He wondered if he had brought a pencil.

Ms. Jackson had kindly given the new boy in her class one of the most interesting animals to study. Now she led her other students off through the bright May morning toward the zebras, the monkeys, the gazelles. Today, each child would choose an animal to observe. In the next few weeks they would do research and write their reports. That was the plan.

But Ms. Jackson never found out what her assignment meant for James. She barely noticed that he was sleepy the next morning, Wednesday. When he was absent Thursday and Friday, she did make some calls. But later, when the principal stopped her in the hall to say James had left the school, Ms. Jackson said only, "Foster children have such a hard time! They go as suddenly as they come." Then she hurried in to hush her class and never thought of James again.

Too bad for Ms. Jackson. The story of what happened after she suggested James take an elephant to study was far more interesting than the reports handed in by any of her other students.

CLICK

After his class left, James glanced around. The elephant yard was as large as the school playground. Just inside the metal fence was a dry moat six feet deep and six feet across. Here and there were thick logs and stumps, some tubs, a tire hanging on a sturdy chain. The elephants didn't interest James. Big old things, just standing there, just another subject in another school. What did elephants have to do with him?

Their bath done, Menika and Beverly came toward the front of the yard. Their ears moved like fans, gently waving with each step. They walked so closely, side by side, James could hear the scrape of their rough skins rubbing together.

Almost at the moat, the elephants stopped. They punched at the ground with their front feet, chopping up hunks of earth and pounding it to dust. With their trunks they swept the dust into little piles, then used their feet to push some into their curled trunk tips. Whipping their trunks around, they threw dust over their backs, under their bellies, against their sides.

1

Earth tumbled off their backs like landslides and floated off in small brown clouds.

The woman with the microphone explained that elephants use dust to keep cool and to protect themselves from the sun. "Their skin is very sensitive. Menika and Beverly are the National Zoo's Asian elephants, from Sri Lanka and India. Daisy, there, our African elephant, is from Zimbabwe." For the first time, James noticed an elephant standing near the fence at the back of the yard.

"You'll notice that African elephants have much larger ears than Asian elephants," the woman said. "All male elephants have visible tusks, but only African females do. Daisy's tusks are small because she's young. She came to Washington, D.C., just a few months ago."

Though she was smaller than the older, Asian, elephants, Daisy seemed bigger, or wilder, to James. Maybe it was the way she was holding her head high with her huge ears forward, or because her trunk curled up in front of her face in an S shape, moving, moving, this way and that.

"Daisy's smelling the air," the woman said. "She seems to have caught a whiff of something in the wind. Elephants can smell things from a long distance away."

The woman began talking about Menika and Beverly again, but James was still watching as Daisy dropped her trunk and walked toward the far corner of the yard. She stopped by a wooden gate blocking the way onto a bridge that crossed the dry moat from the yard to the fence outside. The bridge, just wide enough to hold a truck, was sturdy, and the gate was sturdy, too, with a metal bar along the top. A second gate guarded the outside end of the bridge.

Daisy reached her trunk over the inside gate and with the tip began feeling it up and down. *Chunk!* She whacked it hard.

Suddenly she pulled her trunk in and stood still. James could tell that her body was tense. A keeper was coming by, shoveling up elephant dung, dumping it into a wagon. When the keeper left, Daisy's trunk went back over the gate.

Whatever this elephant was doing with that gate, James was sure she was doing it on purpose, and sure she didn't want her keeper to know. He moved slowly toward her along the path. *Chunk!* Daisy whacked the gate again.

James noticed that her trunk tip always stopped by a flat metal plate on the outside of the gate. He guessed that the plate covered the gate's lock. Could an elephant know that? He crouched behind some bushes and crept closer.

Over and over, Daisy ran the tip of her trunk along the gate, down and up, onto the lock plate, pressing it sideways, then pressing underneath the plate, over and over again. Just once, she paused to smell the high air.

After a few minutes' watching, James looked away beyond the trees of the zoo park, trying to pick out the building where he lived now. He knew the apartment was near the zoo. James's first evening there, Bill had pointed out some big birds, wild birds, flying in to roosts they had made near the zoo's big outdoor bird cage. Martha said they would go to the zoo some weekend, but James had lived there three weekends already, and they hadn't gone.

A new sound—a soft click—made him look back at Daisy. Peeking through the leaves, he saw her push the gate open, just slightly, no more than an inch. Then, with the underside of her trunk, she bumped it closed again. *Click.*

James glanced at the keepers. One was up on Beverly now, just sitting on top of an elephant! The other keeper sat on a stool, filing the bottom of Menika's left rear foot. The woman with the microphone explained that since zoo elephants don't walk nearly as much as elephants in the wild, their feet must be filed down to keep them healthy. Neither keeper was paying any attention to Daisy.

Fast shadows flickered above the bushes. James ducked. Heavy objects, one, then another, tumbled through the leaves just a few feet away from him, hitting the ground softly.

He looked quickly at Daisy who was just swinging her trunk back between her legs. She didn't seem to have noticed him. He held as still as if he were witnessing a crime and, in a way, he was. This elephant—he could hardly believe it!—must have broken off the lock, then thrown it into the bushes. The metal plate was still in place, but underneath it, James was sure, the lock was gone.

Again, Daisy nudged the gate: open—and *click*. She stretched her trunk toward the bushes and sucked in a great breath. The trunk tip turned toward where the heavy things had fallen, then away, still sucking air.

Now, slowly, her ears swung forward, like TV satellite dishes turning to tune in any sound. As her ears spread and her head rose, Daisy seemed to grow, taller, wider, huge! Her trunk tip stopped moving, pointing straight at James. She was smelling him, and she was enormous.

As if he were guilty of something himself, James slowly stood.

Daisy snorted out the air she had breathed in. She observed him for a long moment, then she waved her ears, just slightly.

James sensed, like an urgent call he couldn't quite hear, a low rumble. He didn't feel the elephant was threatening him. Rather, she seemed to be asking him a question. He knew what she needed to know. Just slightly, he shook his head.

Daisy swung a front foot back and forth, as if she wasn't sure what to do. She stared at his face. She moved her ears and her trunk away, then toward him, asking her question again.

James stooped and reached beneath the bushes, groping until he found the pieces of the lock—he knew it would be the lock! He put them in his pocket, stood, shook his head to Daisy even more firmly, then started away. Every few steps, he turned to see what she was doing.

She still smelled him, listened, watched. She took a few steps along the dry moat as if to follow. Then she waggled her ears quickly, like a signal to a friend, and whirled away. She strode to the back of the yard, where she threw a storm of dust over her back.

When he was out of sight of the elephant yard, down by the rhinoceroses, James found a pencil stub in his pocket. He opened his notebook and drew the moat, the bridge, the gate, and a broken lock. After a minute, he wrote, "Why?"

Then he remembered that Ms. Jackson might ask to see his notes. He tore off the page, folded it, and jammed it into his pocket. Before he rejoined his class, he threw the pieces of lock into a trash can. As surely as if he had spoken words she could understand, James had promised Daisy he would keep her secret.

A MYSTERIOUS SHADOW

That afternoon and evening were like every afternoon and evening since James had come to live with Martha and Bill, three weeks before. What was new happened in the night.

As soon as James had dropped his backpack, he went into the bathroom, took off his left sneaker, and stood on the padded floral cover of the toilet seat. With his right knee resting on the sink, he was able to reach the medicine cabinet, take out the can of shaving foam, and squirt some on the back of his hand. James never took much; he hadn't lived here long enough to know what Bill and Martha would do when they got mad. He rubbed the foam into his skin until it disappeared, but he knew the good smell would last, would be there whenever he wanted it, all afternoon.

Climbing down, James was careful not to look in the mirror. His hair was still too short from his last haircut at the group home, a place where children who had no families to live with could stay until they went to a foster family. James never wanted to see that haircut again.

He walked around the kitchen, the living room, their bedroom, his bedroom. In the long afternoons, James had explored it all: the bathroom cabinet, the kitchen cabinets and drawers, the tops and the bottoms and the far-backs of the closets, the magazines and bills lying around. The apartment was crowded with neat furniture, with little pillows on the chairs and little statues on the tables. Only the couch in front of the TV was really comfortable. There wasn't much interesting here. Still, it was a real home.

"Take a deep breath, James, my friend," Karen Grande, his social worker, had said the day she brought him here. "I think this will work out. These are quiet people, a little older." Karen said she'd told them James was a quiet boy and wouldn't make trouble.

"No way I'll make trouble!" he had told Karen. "I'm not going back." It wasn't bad at the group home. The staff was nice, but he didn't know them, and he didn't like living in a place so noisy and crowded.

The best thing in Martha and Bill's apartment, besides the shaving foam, was the big map of Washington and its suburbs above the kitchen table. Bill was a cab driver, and when he was there for a meal, he liked James to test him. James would name a street far from the easy tourist places like the Capitol and the Lincoln Memorial, and Bill would see how fast he could find it. It was fun at first, but James had begun to suspect this was all Bill could think of to talk about with him.

Martha talked to James plenty. She worked in the men's shirts and ties department of a big store, and she loved to tell stories about her fussy customers. One Saturday, she said, she and James would go buy him some clothes on her employee discount.

He'd be glad of that! He didn't have many clothes, and most of them were too big. Someone had sent clothes over to the home for him, clothes chosen more by age than by size, and James was small for his age. He'd been sick when he was a baby, Karen Grande said, which had made him hard to adopt when his mother couldn't keep him after he was born. That's how he had gotten started in foster care.

At the kitchen table, James opened his backpack and pulled out his books. He did the math easily—his new class wasn't up to where his old class had been. He wrote rhymes and definitions for the language-arts words Ms. Jackson had written on the board.

Then he opened *Animals of Africa* to the elephant pages. He was supposed to copy out three facts, but he became so interested, he read right through. He had to go back to find his facts: *Elephants walk about twenty-five miles a day. Elephants eat leaves, grass, fruit, and bark. Their eyesight is weak, but they have strong senses of smell and hearing. They can hear each other calling for over two miles.*

Weak eyesight? James remembered how that zoo elephant had stared at him, after she had opened her gate. He was sure she'd seen him when he shook his head to show he wouldn't tell. Maybe her sight was weak, but it had been a long time since someone had looked back at James like that—understanding him with her eyes.

He put away his books and wandered around the apartment again. If elephants usually walked twenty-five miles a day, maybe that elephant took off her lock so she could go for a nice long walk!

When he heard Martha's key in the lock, James hurried to his room. He liked to be in his own place when she came, ready to smile when she passed his door wearing her fancy black suit, carrying her department-store bag. Some days, she seemed surprised to see him, as if she'd forgotten there was a boy living in her home now. But tonight, as always, she smiled and said, "Evening, James." When her bedroom door closed, James went to wait in the kitchen, enjoying the spicy smell of his shaving foam.

Martha came in, wearing sneakers, white pants, and a bright-red shirt. "Look what I've got!" She held up some carry-out fried chicken. She looked in the fridge, in the freezer, on the shelves. Martha made the same things over and over, and James played his silent game of guessing what she'd choose tonight.

"How about creamed corn and that tomato salad to go with it?"

He nodded. "Popcorn, too?" He loved using the microwave.

"Long as you have your vegetables and milk, sugar." Martha was strict about vegetables and milk. That was one of her mother rules: eat his vegetables and milk, dress neatly for school, do his homework, take a bath, get back on time if he went out, say a nice hello to her friends at church. That was all she asked of James. It was easy.

As she put supper together, Martha talked about her job, about a customer who had taken fifteen minutes deciding between a red tie and a dark-red tie. She told about putting out special items for Father's Day. "Maybe Saturday, we'll go down and get you a nice Father's Day present for Bill."

James didn't say much until she asked about school. "We went to the zoo," he said.

"Those hollering monkeys like to drive me wild!"

James smiled. The shrieks and howls from the gibbons had scared him his first morning here. "I'm studying an elephant."

"Elephants are real calm," Martha said. "I like an elephant. You do your homework?" When he nodded, she fixed them each a tray. "Come on, we'll watch together." Martha had told James she and Bill had signed up to be foster parents because their church had a program. James thought maybe it was because she wanted company watching her stories when Bill got in late.

Martha and Bill used their VCR for two things. Every Saturday night Bill rented a movie, and every weekday Martha recorded the stories, the soap operas that were on while she was at work. Every evening she watched them from beginning to end while she ate supper and did her nails and mended her clothes. James liked sitting next to her on the couch, eating and watching the stories.

He loved how—no matter where he lived—the people in the stories kept having their fights and their problems and their romances. He hadn't seen those shows all the weeks he'd been at the group home, after he had left Big Jim and Yolanda's. When Martha had turned on the VCR his first evening here, he'd felt like he was seeing old friends. It made Martha happy to find out he knew the stories so well.

James had soon discovered he had one problem, though: Martha always sent him to do his homework when *This Old World* came on. It was like one of her mother rules. Did she think that show wasn't good for him? Did she think he didn't know the bad stuff that could happen? One good thing about Yolanda, she hadn't cared what he watched.

James had begun doing his homework in the afternoon, hoping Martha would let him watch the show. She started sending him to have his bath, instead. But he left the bathroom door open a crack, and in the tub he listened to the *This Old World* people screaming and loving, and to Martha racing through the ads with fast forward. As quickly as he washed, he never made it out until the program was almost over.

He had thought of taking his baths in the afternoon, too, but if Martha thought he was messing with her, she might send him back to the home. Tonight when *This Old World* came on, he just said, "I used to watch that with my other foster mother."

"That story's not fit for a child only ten years old," Martha said. "I hardly watch it myself. Go on, have your bath, sugar. You'll still have one nice story, after."

After the last show, James went to read his book in bed. He knew Martha wouldn't do anything now but talk to her friends and fall asleep. He said good-night before she picked up the phone, so she'd have time to say something nice back to him.

James's bedroom was crowded. Besides his bed, there was a table with three lamps on it, four old chairs, and some cardboard cartons stacked against the walls. He kept everything he'd brought in two drawers of the bureau, though Martha had said he could use them all. He liked to keep his things tight together.

Before he climbed into bed, James reached under his shirts and pulled out his red sock. He shook out his coins and bills. He had started saving at his first foster home, where he got paid for doing chores. At his last home, Yolanda would give him a quarter to be quiet when she wanted a nap. At the group home, the staff sometimes gave out money for candy, and sometimes James saved his. Even Karen Grande didn't know about James's money. He counted it every night, though the amount—$31.20—hadn't changed for weeks. He wasn't getting any money here, yet. Still, $31.20 might be enough, if something happened.

Late in the night, James had a dream so mean it woke him.

He didn't call out. He used to call to Big Jim when he had his dreams. Big Jim would come check out the room, and then he'd talk, first telling jokes to make James happy, then sweet stories to help James back to sleep. The first night here, James had been too shy to call out. When he called the second night, Bill came in and told him everything was fine and to go back to sleep. James could do that for himself.

A streetlamp stood outside his window, and since the apartment was on the second floor the light shone right in. James tried to take comfort from it now, but he couldn't lose the feeling of his dream—a feeling of being locked up, alone. He smelled his hand, but the smell of Bill's shaving foam—of Big Jim's shaving foam—was gone.

He could never remember exactly the reasons why he couldn't go back to Big Jim, though Karen Grande had explained, had told him about her guidelines for foster homes. James almost never asked her about Big Jim anymore; still, he thought about him.

He jerked his head away from his pillow as if to jerk

his mind away from that dream. His clock said two in the morning. He went over to the window, took out the screen, and leaned into the soft, cool air of the night.

No one was outside. The only cars were parked and empty. The buildings and sidewalks, even the leaves and signs that would have been brightly colored in sunlight, were all washed to gray. The doorways and the alley across the street, where no light fell, were black shadows.

The street was so peaceful, so strange, James wanted to be part of it. He climbed onto the windowsill and sat sideways, one leg dangling outside almost down to the bushes. Martha would probably say this was dangerous. James smiled—he knew he never did anything really dangerous. His hands were holding tight.

Then he saw something move. Across the street, down at the end of the block, a huge shadow slithered over the building fronts and stoops, jiggling in and out of the windows and doorways. It seemed to James the shadow of a hulking beast of prey, or of a spaceship coming in to land.

For a long moment, he couldn't tell what was making the shadow. Then, as if all at once his eyes had learned to see, there was an elephant, an elephant pounding down the sidewalk as if it were on the most important mission in the world.

NIGHTWALKERS

James stared, astonished. This had to be that African elephant from the zoo. She must have broken the lock on the bridge's outside gate too, and now here she was, coming down his block. But this was wrong—an elephant loose in the city!

Her feet made no sound, and her gray blended into the night colors of the street. James had to strain to see her moving just ahead of, then just behind, her own black shadow as she passed a streetlamp. Only her small tusks gleamed brightly.

She didn't seem to be looking for him, hurrying on as she was, but James couldn't take a chance. He scrambled back inside. When he looked out again, the elephant had passed the alley across from his building—and she had stopped.

She turned her head, ears out, toward his side of the street, as if she'd been surprised by sudden news. Her trunk curved high in the S salute James had seen at the zoo, and an S curved up from the shadow behind her. The trunk tip moved, like a submarine's periscope searching, until it pointed straight at his window.

James stepped back into the darkness, but he knew he couldn't hide whatever smell he had. The elephant turned to face the way she had been going. "Go *on*," James whispered. "Keep going. Go on!"

After a long moment, she seemed to make up her mind. In all his life, James had never seen anything so big coming at him! He ran behind his bed and lay flat on the floor, hardly breathing, pretending he wasn't there.

He told himself she hadn't come to his street to find him. Then why, if she was in such a hurry, after she noticed him had she changed her mind and come across? His book said elephants had good memories: In times of little rain, an old mother could lead her family to waterholes it hadn't used in many years. Maybe this elephant remembered that James knew the secret of her busted lock. Was she angry that he knew? Had she understood when he shook his head? Or was she thinking some other, elephant, kind of thing?

He heard the windy sound of an elephant smelling. He peeked over the bed. Her trunk was reaching up and over his windowsill. When the trunk faced him precisely, it stretched toward him, and the sound of her smelling grew louder.

James listened toward the hall. Martha would hate this animal trunk snuffling into her clean apartment! If she saw one cockroach while she fixed supper, she mentioned it all evening. Well, *he* had not invited the elephant in.

Whoosh! She blew out the air she had sucked in, and, just as at the zoo, James sensed her low rumble. Again this elephant had smelled him out, again he felt she needed something from him. He didn't want her making one of those elephant trumpet sounds in here. Once again he stood for her inspection, and this time, though his legs trembled, he walked toward her.

As soon as she could touch him, she wrapped her trunk around his arm. The trunk was thick, muscular as a snake, but wrinkled and with many stiff black hairs, some longer than James's finger. He felt its ridges flex against his skin as the elephant pulled him toward her. When he tried to resist, she kept right on pulling as if she didn't notice. But though her trunk was the strongest live thing that had ever touched him, it didn't hurt at all.

When she had him against the windowsill, her trunk tip moved over his body, sucking in smells from his feet, his pajamas, his ears. She smelled long and hard at his mouth. Did his breath smell bad? He had brushed his teeth. Maybe she liked the new green toothpaste Martha had bought. He couldn't taste it anymore, but maybe an elephant could smell it.

Just smelling, the elephant seemed so calm, James was less frightened. When she pulled on him again, though, he panicked: There was no place to go but out the window!

He realized this was the way he'd felt when Karen Grande had come to the group home to take him to live with Martha and Bill: He had been frightened about where he would be taken, but he couldn't stop it from happening. All his life, James had gone where other people wanted him to go. He had gotten used to it—and this elephant trunk was so strong. He climbed out the window now.

The elephant guided him down till he was sitting on her neck, his legs hanging down behind her ears, which folded back to cover them as she started off. Her first great stride seemed to roll her back right out from underneath him. He grabbed on to her ears and tried not to look at the ground.

The elephant was going in the same direction as when James had first seen her, her back flowing and dipping toward one side, then the other. Riding her reminded him of playing on the water bed when Yolanda wasn't home. Still, this was no game. The broad streets were gray and empty. He saw no one, no one at all. Who would hear him if he called?

At the corner by a wide avenue, though the light was green and there were no cars moving, the elephant stopped. As she spread her ears, cool air swirled over James's legs. She raised her trunk in all directions. She had not stopped to check the traffic lights, he realized. She was checking signals *she* could understand: smells and sounds. How strange an elephant was, how different from a human! But she might know words, like those other elephants did. What was her name? Daisy? He tried it: "Daisy!"

Immediately, her trunk rose up and pointed back toward him. Inside, it was divided into two holes, like huge human nostrils. This big long thing wasn't a hose, he remembered, it was a nose. At the end were the two tips she used to pick things up, which his book called "fingers." Daisy used them now to gently squeeze his arm. Then she swung her trunk down, turned right, and went running down a long hill, racing almost gaily, like a kid at recess.

She'd answered when he said her name! Could he command her as the keepers did? James wondered, but he didn't care. He didn't have anything for her to do, or anyplace he needed her to go.

Hugging himself to keep warm, laughing out loud, James found he wasn't worried any longer. Daisy's neck was so broad he was in no danger of falling. It didn't matter that he didn't know where she was going. He trusted her. Far down the block, someone was walking quickly, with his head down. But James had no need to call anyone but Daisy.

Though the ride was smooth, Daisy's stiff hairs pricked through his pajamas. Her strong smell might have been bad too, if James hadn't liked it so much. He was surrounded by her smell. He could almost feel it, heavy on his skin, stuffing up inside his nose. It was sweet and musty, like the smell in the barn for U.S. Park Police horses where he'd gone once on a school trip.

At the bottom of the hill, she stopped again, trunk up. James heard a faraway siren. Daisy paid it no attention, and it died away into a deep silence. In the apartment houses, almost every window was dark.

Daisy went on, stopped again, listened, and moved under a tree. A little breeze rustled the leaves by James's head, but Daisy stood absolutely still. A car sped past. The driver never noticed them, and in a minute she started again.

Daisy seemed born to be a secret nightwalker in the city. She knew when a car was coming long before James saw headlights or heard a motor. Soon he had learned to lie low against her whenever she hid in an alley or under the shadow of a tree, to hide, as much as possible, his bright pajamas.

Wherever two streets crossed, Daisy stopped to test the air. Sometimes she stopped on the sidewalk, sometimes not until she was in the middle of the street. Sometimes James sensed a rumble as if she were sending out a question. He couldn't tell if she heard any answer. When she was ready, she went on, whether the light was red or green or blinking yellow.

After many blocks, she crossed a grassy area to the edge of the Potomac River and stopped at the rail. Her trunk stretched far out over the water. Could she smell all the way across to Virginia? Probably not, James thought, for the air was still now. He hoped she didn't plan to cross the river. If she started whacking down the rail, he was going to jump right off! He knew elephants could swim, but he was pretty sure he could not.

Daisy didn't try to cross. Soon her body relaxed, her trunk fell, and her ears lay flat over James's legs. When she turned away from the river, she was going more slowly. She didn't stop at corners, she didn't smell the air, as if she didn't care so much now where she went.

After a few blocks, she crossed a curving street into a little park shaped like a circle. There she moved from tree to tree, reaching up, tearing off fresh spring leaves and jamming them into her mouth. She snapped off whole branches, chomping the leaves and twigs, tossing away the part she couldn't eat. Her slow chewing made the leaves sound juicy and delicious.

In the center of the park, high on a pedestal, was a statue of a man on a horse. The word "Washington" was carved below. Probably, James thought, this was the great George Washington. The statue horse looked surprised, even frightened, as if it really could see an elephant feeding herself in its park.

Up on Daisy, he might be able to reach the horse's leg, maybe even touch George Washington's toe. He tugged her ear in that direction. She didn't move. She was eating flowers from neatly planted rows now, lifting them to her mouth one by one, crunching blossom, stalk, leaves, roots, and most of the dirt as well.

Suddenly she swung around and flung a flower smack against the horse. She stood, head high, ears spreading, puffing herself up, challenging the statue.

Again she yanked up a flower and—*whomp!*—hit the horse. Again she watched it. Then she waggled her ears and lifted her trunk to pull her next mouthful from the trees.

James stared at the statue, trying to figure out if an elephant could tell it was a horse. He stared at the flowerbed that now had holes where half the plants had been. Did she know what a mess she had made?

When Daisy moved under some low hanging branches, James lay flat and soon he heard a siren, coming closer, closer, almost unbearably loud. An ambulance circled the park and stopped under a wide roof with EMERGENCY MEDICINE written on it. Some people jumped down, took out a stretcher bed with someone on it, and rolled it inside.

That tall building, with so many lights on so late, was a hospital, a hospital James realized that he knew. He had been there just a few months ago, on the worst night of his life. He had to look inside now.

When he slid off her back, Daisy's skin, rough as tree bark, and her stiff hair scratched his belly. The ground was farther down than he'd expected. His bare feet tingled when they hit. It was a minute before he could start moving cautiously toward the emergency room entrance. He barely wondered whether Daisy would be there when he got back. He had to take the chance. As he knelt behind a bush at the edge of the park, he could see wheelchairs inside the wide glass doors, as he remembered, and someone in green clothes hurrying down the bright hall.

He and Big Jim had stayed here all night, the last time Yolanda went in. She'd been in trouble with drugs once before. That first time, Big Jim had had to talk and talk so Karen Grande wouldn't take James away. The second time, he and Big Jim had sat here waiting, hardly talking at all. They each knew James would not be allowed to stay now—with Yolanda, if she got out, or with Big Jim alone. As the hospital clock had moved from nine to ten to midnight and beyond, Big Jim's arm lay heavy along James's shoulder, and the brim of his cap was pulled down, hiding his face.

Before James could cross the street to look inside, the ambulance people came out, folding down their roller bed, putting it in, slamming the doors. Their voices echoed off the roof above the driveway.

That hospital entrance, James realized, was no place for him. Even when these people left, someone else might see him peeking through the glass doors and ask what he was doing there, a kid alone so late at night. He couldn't say he hoped Big Jim might somehow still—almost three months later!—be in the waiting room, waiting for him.

As he walked back, Daisy loomed ahead, a huge shadow ripping apart the shadowy trees. He approached her slowly, until her trunk reached out and gently pulled him near.

She was so big! Even her eyelashes were enormous, long and thick, like black plastic spaghetti. The creases in her skin were so deep and wide he could have poked his finger in. As he stood next to Daisy she seemed to James the only other creature in the world. Everything his eyes saw, every smell his nose smelled, all his ears heard, all he touched was Daisy. Even the air around him had a taste of elephant!

She brushed a branch of leaves across his face. The most amazing part of all was that this huge animal seemed to be James's friend.

But how was he going to get up there, up on her back again, so high? "Daisy? Come! Up! Go!" He hoped she knew one of those words. "Help! Up! Carry! Lift!"

He must have said something she understood. She folded her front leg to make a step for him and gave him a boost with her trunk. He grabbed her ear, and after a moment's awkward scramble, he was up.

Already, her head was back amid the leaves. She seemed to have forgotten he was there. Martha had said elephants are calm. For a few minutes more, Daisy went on calmly ruining the park.

When she finally left, ambling off with a leafy twig stuck between her tusk and her trunk, James could stay awake no longer. It must be almost morning. He was supposed to get up in a couple of hours! He put his head down on top of hers, with a hand underneath so his face wouldn't rub against her skin.

Later, he felt her bumping down a slope and heard gurgling sounds. He looked around. The sky was lighter now. They were in woods, with birdsong all around. Daisy had found a creek. She drank four or five trunkfuls of water, then started sloshing along as if the creek were her private road through the park. James closed his eyes again.

When he was awakened by the familiar early-morning howling of the gibbons, he found that the creek had led them to the zoo. Daisy didn't go to the elephant house, but hurried up the other hill to James's street.

There, she quickly moved beneath a tree. Her neck vibrated as a garbage truck rumbled past. Then she walked to his window, and he hauled himself in, tumbling to the floor. When he looked out again, she was gone.

Tired as he was, James couldn't sleep. He remembered the question he had written at the zoo. He still did not know why Daisy had busted her lock, why she had wanted to get out. She had seemed to be going toward something, looking for something, something more than leaves and flowers to eat, but what that could be, he didn't know.

SOMEONE TO SEARCH FOR

When his alarm rang an hour and a half later, James wished he could sleep late, like Bill. After he had gotten dressed—slowly pulling on each sock, slowly tying each sneaker—he sat for a moment trying to believe he had ridden an elephant out into the night.

At breakfast, with his spoon dripping milk halfway to his mouth, he stared at Bill's map. A thin blue line, Rock Creek, ran by the zoo and down not far from Washington Circle to the Potomac River. But that didn't mean James had ridden along Rock Creek on an elephant.

Martha finished pouring her coffee. "Sugar, are you sure you took a *good* bath last night?"

Before he could be careful, before he could hold in his grin, James's question burst out: "I smell?"

"Now, don't smile! You know it's important to take a good bath. You don't want to go to school smelling like that."

Of *course* he smelled. He smelled of Daisy! "I'll take a good bath tonight," he promised. But as soon as

Martha left, he scrubbed his hands, his feet, and his stomach where he had rubbed against Daisy's skin as he slid off. He *didn't* want to go to school smelling like an elephant.

On his way, he stooped and read the headlines showing through the windows of the blue and orange newspaper boxes. He saw no news about an elephant escaping from the zoo or about a smashed-up park. But James knew that none of the important things that happened to him had ever got in the newspaper or on TV. Yet they had happened.

Maybe no newspaper news about Daisy's escape meant no one else had found out: Maybe she'd gone back to the zoo, and into the elephant yard, and closed both gates behind her. That would be the most amazing news of all—but no one would know except James.

The day was very long. Too sleepy, too confused about Daisy to study or hear what Ms. Jackson said, James stared at pictures in his Africa book, pictures of elephants washing and drinking in a river, of an elephant mother scaring away hyenas while her baby stood close by.

Walking from school, he had to cross the street to avoid a man he didn't like. He had seen Howard Thomas three or four times since he had moved here, hanging out in a store parking lot with some other men. James never wanted to say even hello to him. He used to hate it when Big Jim brought Howard home for something to eat. He never understood why Big Jim was so kind to rude Howard.

When he came to his apartment building, James walked right by. He had to find out about Daisy. He walked down the hill, across the bridge over Rock Creek, and uphill again to the elephant house. Lucky this zoo is free, he thought.

Daisy was there! She stood in the yard with the other elephants, looking as if she had never left. James leaned on the rail to watch. The elephants seemed to be dozing in the warm sun. Their bodies were still, but usually some other part was moving: an ear flapping, a long, pointy mouth flopping open, a foot swinging, a tail whisking legs, a trunk searching the ground.

James wondered if Daisy would go out again tonight, and if she would come for him. Probably she wouldn't. She was paying no more attention to him now than Menika and Beverly were, though once he thought she lifted her trunk in his direction. Soon he was so sleepy, he almost didn't care.

"They're big, I *know* that! They're big, and they stink!" A little kid was talking to a woman. "They're big, and they stink, and that's *all*! Let's go see the octopus."

James made himself stand up again. The elephants were hardly boring to him now! The longer he watched them, the more he saw.

One of the keepers put down a bale of hay. The elephants soon gathered around, and he watched how they divided it: First, Menika whacked the bale, breaking it up. As she started to eat, Beverly reached over and pulled away a portion much smaller than half. When Daisy tried for a piece of that, Beverly pushed it out of her reach. When Daisy finally got some hay, it was not even half of Beverly's small half.

James could tell who was boss in this herd! But did Daisy get so little because she was youngest, or because she was smallest, or because she was new? His head sunk down again onto his hands, which were resting on the rail.

A few minutes later he looked up and Daisy was right there, across the moat. She did remember him! Her trunk flicked out at him, and, as he had the night before, James sensed that she wanted, needed, something badly.

He wondered why his book called her eyes weak when they seemed to stare at him so hard. When he looked back at her, it was almost a conversation. As if they *had* talked, he was absolutely sure she would be going out tonight. He was almost sure, as well, that she meant him to be part of it, part of whatever it was she was doing, nightwalking through the city.

Daisy's ears went flat against her head. A keeper was coming along the dry moat, picking up trash. Hoping Daisy wouldn't be insulted, he moved away.

"You like elephants?" the keeper said as James passed.

"Yeah." He didn't want questions, and he did want a nap. He kept right on going. When he turned for a last look at Daisy, she was over by her freedom gate. "See you tonight!" James whispered it like a prayer.

Going up the hill, he thought about how she had walked out in the night with such strong purpose, pounding along on a carefully chosen way. What could an elephant care so much about, in a city? She must be searching for something. The woman at the zoo had said Daisy was new. Maybe she was trying to find the place where she used to live.

I have something I could search for, James thought. Someone. If Daisy took him with her again, he would look out for Big Jim's place. He knew he shouldn't keep hoping about Big Jim. Karen Grande always said to make the best of what he had. She said he had a good home now.

Howard would know about Big Jim! Howard Thomas, standing around, leaning on cars—Howard could tell him. Once again, James passed right by his building.

Four men were with Howard in the parking lot today and one of them was talking, telling a story so slowly James could hardly follow it. He watched from a little way off, waiting for the man's voice to stop. He noticed that one of Howard's eyes was more open than the other and his hands shook when he tried to button his coat.

The man never did stop talking, even when the others interrupted him. Finally James stepped closer. "Howard?"

"Who's calling me Howard?" Howard asked sharply.

A small man laughed harshly. "He knows you, Howard! He's got you now!"

"James, is it!" Howard said. "How you doin', James?"

"Okay." James didn't ask how Howard was doing. He could see that for himself.

"How's that little Big Jim of yours?" Howard asked.

The small man whooped and clapped his hands. "Lord, have mercy!"

"I'm not with Big Jim anymore," James said. "Don't *you* see him?"

"I don't see him *now*!" Howard's laugh was loud and mean, and all the others echoed it.

"Well, do you know how he's doing?" James didn't know why these men would laugh about Big Jim. He hated it that his questions gave them a chance to laugh, but he needed to know. "Where he's working now? Is he still living where he was?"

"I don't *ever* see him, now he's at his mama's! I'm not welcome in his mama's house! Oh, no! I guess he likes to stay there." Howard was almost shouting now, talking more to his friends than to James. "I guess he likes to get his room free, even if he has to eat out every night!" Howard didn't notice when James said good-bye and walked away.

James had to smile. Mama *was* a terrible cook. But Howard didn't know Mama was really Big Jim's aunt, and James didn't tell him. He wasn't surprised Big Jim was at Mama's. Just before James left, with Yolanda already gone to her treatment center, Big Jim had said he might go live with Mama.

James had loved hearing Howard say the name—even so rudely. It seemed to make Big Jim real again. Their names were alike, Big Jim had said, only by coincidence, and he explained to James what that meant: Their names were the same only by chance.

Big Jim had loved to tell how everything about his own name was wrong. He wasn't big, or tough either, the way his name sounded. He wasn't even Jim. His name was Stanley, but when he left school to get a job, he told people he was Big Jim. As if, he had always said, he was getting ready for James to come, getting ready to be James's father.

How James longed for Big Jim!

Maybe he would call Big Jim at Mama's. Maybe. He could. He had that number. Another foster kid had once told him to take all the phone numbers before he left any place he lived, in case sometime he had to call. James kept his numbers with his money in his red sock.

But Big Jim had never come to see him at the group home, the way he said he would, and James had never called. Maybe he would call now. He would like just to talk. Big Jim was great at talking. Maybe James would call. Probably he wouldn't. Probably talking to mean Howard was easier than calling Big Jim and having to find out why he had never come.

When he unlocked the apartment door, he didn't

look at the phone. He turned on the TV and flopped down on the couch, knowing he should do his homework, too sleepy to do anything but punch the remote control.

If Daisy came tonight, he thought dreamily, maybe she would take him near Mama's house. Maybe he'd hear Big Jim in the basement playing Ping-Pong, shouting after a great shot, or see him on the porch talking with his friends. Maybe James could make Daisy go near, so Big Jim could see her. Big Jim would love Daisy!

A knock on the door woke him like an alarm.

FF AND THE FFF

James stood up slowly, and, without remembering to ask who was there, he opened the door. Luckily, it was Karen Grande, in a bright yellow dress. Unluckily, he would have to stay awake.

"So how are you?" Karen asked, dropping her shoulder sack on the floor with a thud.

James shrugged and slumped onto the couch.

Karen looked at him carefully. "Ms. Jackson says you were only half there in school today." She waited another minute. "Sleepy?"

"She's not very interesting," James said. "I don't like it as much as that other school." Karen had tried, and failed, to keep him in the same schools the last two times he'd moved.

"You really liked Ms. McKenna, didn't you?"

James nodded. "She really liked me. She always said hello, every morning. Right to me."

"Well, give Ms. Jackson a little time to find out what a great kid you are."

James grinned back at her as if they had a secret.

"Is there a funny smell in here?" Karen looked around.

James lowered his eyes. He didn't smell anything.

"Maybe it's out on the street." Karen returned to more professional questions: "Is something keeping you up late?"

"No," James said carefully. "I go to bed early."

"Do you hear your family? Do they keep you awake?"

"They don't fight or anything. They don't do anything." He sat up. "You think I could go live with Big Jim? Sometime?"

"You know the answer to that, James." Karen leaned over and searched in her sack among her folders and her papers.

"I know where he is now. He's at his aunt's."

"Have you seen him?"

James heard the sharpness in her question and quickly shook his head. "Somebody told me. How long am I going to stay here?"

"A good while, I hope." Karen opened her notebook as she began talking in her easy way, asking about his new family. Did he like them? Yeah. Did he like their friends? How was the food? Good! He described the fried chicken Martha had brought last night. What did he do last weekend? How did he like school? Did he have any friends in school yet?

James didn't think much about friends anymore. He had liked a few kids at his last school, but now he was too far away to see them. He was tired of new people.

Karen was his oldest friend. She had been his social worker for four years. He hadn't known her well while everything was okay, but in the last few months, he had seen her a lot. She had been coming every week, since he moved.

"Why are you asking all that?" He picked up the remote control. "You asked me last week."

"I don't care." Karen grinned her teasing grin. "I don't care about you at all. It's my boss wants to know how you like school."

"You talk to somebody about me?"

"You know I do. I told you."

"When do I have to go see my judge again?"

"Not for a while. Not unless there's some change."

"Am I going to stay here?"

"Do you want to?"

"I don't care." He glanced at the fat bag where Karen kept the folders on her children. James's folder told about his foster care. No one knew anything about his real father, but Karen had told him some about his real mother, and he knew more from over-hearing when his foster families talked. Karen had promised he would know the rest someday. For now, she just wanted him to have a good, stable family, and do good work at school, and have friends.

He lay back against the couch, thinking about his new school. There were some kids he might like, if he stayed. "Ms. Jackson doesn't pay much attention to me. Because"—he shrugged—"you know, I'm good."

Karen laughed. "Don't knock it!" She wrote something down. When James pretended to peek into her notebook, she turned it so he could see.

He was surprised. "I can read it?"

"You can read anything you like."

James stared at her writing. "What's 'FF'? Social-worker code?"

"Fast food."

He giggled. "Because I told about the chicken?"

"I have to watch you on that fast food, James. At Big Jim and Yolanda's you were eating fast food all the time. He was always taking you to the FF places."

"We had to do it, man! It was necessary! No one in that family can cook."

"Hmmm," Karen said. "Someone in that family could have learned."

It's not even a family now, James thought. Nobody together. He didn't know if Yolanda was still in that place. He looked at Karen's notebook again. "Then what's 'FFF'?" He thought a minute. "Fancy fast food? Fried?"

"Former foster father."

"Big Jim?" Once again he sat up straight, wide-awake now. "Did you talk to him?"

Karen shook her head. "Not in a long time. You mentioned him. Remember?"

"Yeah." James stood and looked her in the eye. "I

mention him a lot." He touched the FFF and the FF and said slyly, "All the 'F' words I love."

Karen was trying to look stern, but James could tell she was laughing inside.

"I'm glad you never take me to fast-food places," he said.

"Why?" She sounded surprised.

"Some kids don't like to go there, if their social worker takes them. It means she's transferring them someplace else."

Karen looked at him and nodded once. When she returned to her questions, James interrupted her: "Do you have a newspaper?"

"In my car. Do you need it?"

"Did you read any news about an elephant?"

"No." Karen looked puzzled.

"The zoo is right down the hill from here," James said. "I'm doing a report on one of the elephants."

"There's not usually news about the zoo animals," she said. "Unless they have a baby or something."

"I just wonder if the animals get out." Carefully watching Karen's face, James saw that she was carefully watching his.

"I wouldn't worry, James," she said. "They keep the animals secure." She used her cheerful voice again: "You're lucky to have a zoo close by!"

"I used to be near a library." James had learned as he moved to different homes that, like the stories on television, he could count on the stories in books to remain the same. "I wish I was near a library now."

"Oh, stop moaning!" Karen laughed. "Use the school library. Or get Bill or Martha to show you how to get to one on the bus. Your card's good at any library in the city."

"Anywhere I live?"

"Anywhere you live." She stood up, and her voice was really cheerful now: "So, James! You're doing real well here."

Quickly he looked up at her, then looked away.

"I won't be coming by next week. I'll see you in a couple of weeks. Okay?"

He shrugged. He knew that soon Karen would stop coming much at all.

"Get enough sleep, will you? And give them a chance. They like you. They say you're a good boy. Are you?"

James grinned. "Pretty good."

After he had locked the door behind her, he went in to sit on his bed and wait, for Martha to come, for supper and the shows and the whole evening.

And the night, he reminded himself. He grinned again, thinking about what social-worker code might be for taking a late-night ride on an elephant.

A HUNK OF CONCRETE

That night, getting ready for bed earlier than usual, James carried a dab of the new green toothpaste out of the bathroom on his finger. He called good-night to Martha from the hall, but she was snoring gently, the TV still on. In his room, he smeared the toothpaste on top of his clock, just in case.

Then, just in case, instead of pajamas he put on a gray sweatshirt and brown pants, dark clothes to hide him, heavy pants to protect him against Daisy's hair. Looking at his dark-brown skin, he thought maybe he, too, was born to be a secret nightwalker. He put his sneakers ready by the window, took out the screen, and got into bed, too sleepy even to count the money in his red sock.

Whomp! Something hit him. Turning over, barely awake, James thought he must be in the group home with those tough boys. A *whoosh* of air made him look toward the window. Daisy's trunk was reaching in, and one of his sneakers was on the floor by his bed. Quickly, he licked the toothpaste from the clock—it was almost three!—and ran to the window. "Hello!" he whispered.

Daisy loved the smell. James breathed out, then in and out again, and still she held up her trunk. Supplying enough minty air to satisfy her took more breath than blowing up a partyful of balloons! James was pleased to have figured out a such good present for an elephant.

Suddenly, she was ready to leave, and she pulled him out the window. Her trunk was not rough, but it left him no choice at all—not that he would have chosen to stay.

She started, and as each side of her in turn seemed to pour smoothly from beneath him, James felt at home, safe and calm and sure. Riding Daisy already seemed the usual, for him.

Watching her shadow slide over the building fronts, he noticed above her large shape two smaller round shapes, one above the other. He threw his arms up, and the small shadow did the same. It *was* him! His head, his body, him! James the Elephant Rider! He wished they could go forever.

But the trip was a serious matter for Daisy. She had chosen a new direction, and the strong wind must be bringing her strong signals, for tonight she seemed sure of where she was going. Though she tested the air and rumbled her questions at every corner, she rarely changed her path.

James had begun to believe he lived in a sea of

smells and sounds he knew almost nothing about. There must be a lot to learn, he thought, by smelling and listening when the stink and hubbub of traffic and people were gone. He watched Daisy and tried to understand the city her way. When she put up her trunk, James sniffed the air. When she put out her ears, he listened hard. He learned nothing. All he saw, all around, was the gray-and-black city night, empty.

Once, far off down a wide street, down a long hill, he saw the White House, lit up and glowing in the night. He wished they could go closer. He tugged on Daisy's ear, but really he knew by now that an elephant goes where she wants to go, when she wants to go there, always doing only what she wants to do. Daisy wasn't rumbling her questions to the President. She didn't even turn to look.

Once a taxi slowed as it passed them, and James could see the driver looking around. He and Daisy both held still, and the cab went on, not hurrying away as if the driver had just seen a huge wild beast loose in the city. Just as last night, Daisy was wonderfully careful not to be seen.

She hurried past rows of small painted houses with small front yards, past a Metro station and some schools, past fancy churches and little churches that looked like stores. Some of these places looked familiar to James, as if he might once have lived nearby—when, he wasn't sure.

Coming to another broad avenue, Daisy didn't stop

at all, but crossed eagerly into a small rectangular park. Tall trees and tall lamps followed a path along the park's edge. But in the center, inside a wall of low-hanging branches, was a dark, open field, where dogs might run, or children play, or a band give a concert on a Saturday afternoon. Daisy headed straight for the center.

Her ears were forward, her skinny tail stuck straight out behind, and her body was tense, no longer so comfortable for James. Trunk down, but without plucking one blade of grass, she moved carefully across the field, as if she meant to examine every inch. The park was not so far from the zoo. Since elephants could smell and hear a long way, James thought perhaps some news from here had reached her there. He wished he could help her, but he didn't know what Daisy expected might be here, or might have been here and gone.

He noticed a PLEASE CLEAN UP AFTER YOUR DOG sign, and quickly looked behind them where Daisy had walked. Tomorrow morning, he thought, some kid's going to find that and think somebody didn't clean up after the biggest dog this city ever saw! Wishing someone would come along right now so he could watch them find it, James peered through the leaves toward the street.

Slowly, he became aware of people standing on the other side, just standing, soft as shadows, not moving, not speaking, as gray as the buildings behind them.

Why were they here, so many, so early, so quiet?

He remembered that Big Jim had once told him about "the corner," where people could wait for work in the early, early morning. Builders and landscapers came by in trucks to pick up a crew to work that day. Big Jim was a carpenter, and a good one. Usually, he had a job. But if he ever had to, he had told James, he could go to the corner to get work. James remembered that as his eyes darted over the silent crowd.

Holding down his sweatshirt so his stomach wouldn't scrape, he slid off Daisy. She kept walking, and he walked backward before her, keeping clear of her swinging trunk. "I'll be back in a minute," he told her. "Don't go. Stay."

When he spoke, she held up her trunk. From deep inside, he breathed out a warm breath for her, though he could hardly taste the toothpaste anymore. Daisy took a long smell, then dropped her trunk back to the grass. "Stay." That was dog talk; he hoped she understood.

James saw a man hurry along the edge of the park, then angle off across the street. The man had on a cap like one Big Jim wore, though James knew the man was too tall to be Big Jim. Still James ran after him, hoping somehow this man had news for him. "Mister!"

The man kept going, faster now, not answering, not even turning to look at James until he had crossed and joined the others. James started to follow him, then glanced back at Daisy.

Wildly, softly, she moved within the dark trees. She was so glorious that for a moment James forgot everything to watch her. Even from where he was, the front part of her body seemed enormous: Her legs were so tall and her massive head so high. Her ears were spread, listening through the air. Her trunk swung wide and low, smelling the ground in front of her footsteps. Her silhouette flowed and changed with every step, and whenever she turned, a tusk flashed white.

When at last James made himself cross the street, the man in Big Jim's cap was fumbling with matches, lighting a cigarette, sucking in the smoke. He looked up, startled, at James's voice.

"Mister, do you know a guy named Big Jim? Do you ever see him around here? Big Jim?" James said the name loudly, hoping other people would hear. He was too shy to ask up and down the crowd.

The man shook his head. He wrapped his arms around himself, then unwrapped them and shook his head again.

Then Daisy trumpeted. James's book had said elephants trumpet, and he had no doubt that's what this harsh, ugly screech was. When she was done, the silence was absolute, as if the air must recover from her blast before it could again carry ordinary sound.

A few people stared for a moment at the park's shadowy trees. "Did you hear that?" one man called out. "Was that a horn?" No one answered. The rest of the crowd moved closer together, whispering, looking down the street.

Even from where he was, seeing only glimpses of her through the leaves, James could tell that something had changed for Daisy. She was going over and over the same piece of ground. She would take a few strides, fling up her trunk, then turn around.

James asked the man in the cap, "Do you know if there are animals around here?"

The man took a deep drag on his cigarette, staring at the ground. When he opened his mouth, he coughed and smoke sputtered out.

James stepped back, then asked again, "Like over in that park? Wild animals?"

The crowd murmured and moved, and the man looked up sharply. Far down the street James saw headlights coming. The man dropped his cigarette and stepped on it. "A little circus," he said. "I brought my kids. It left a couple of days ago, going to some mall."

James wanted to ask more, but the man in the cap had already walked away. A truck had stopped, and a man with a clipboard stepped down and began calling out information as the people crowded around.

James raced into the park and right to Daisy, his arms raised, ready to grab her ear. But though she bent her leg up for him to step on, she set it down again. She swung her trunk behind him, as if to give him a boost, then swung it away.

For the first time, he could clearly hear her rumble, deep inside her head like drumbeats, or a woodpecker pecking under water. Her foot swung restlessly. She seemed eager to leave, but she didn't help him up.

When she swung her trunk again, he saw she was holding a piece of pavement, a hunk of rough concrete not much bigger than a grapefruit, set with stones and a rusted bolt. Her problem seemed to be that she didn't know how to boost him and still keep hold of it. She started toward the street.

James followed, shouting, "Daisy! Go! Up!" He couldn't remember which words had worked before. "Lift! Help! Carry!"

She turned and watched him for a moment, then dropped the rubble, stamping her foot on top of it. She helped James onto her back and immediately picked up the concrete again.

He felt vibrations in her neck. When a garbage truck rumbled by a moment later, the vibrations grew stronger and her body tensed, just as when she'd heard a garbage truck the night before. Maybe, James thought, the humped gray trucks seemed to her like strange elephants, huge, swift, and dangerous.

Like a Metro train speeding toward a far-off station, Daisy ran—the opposite way from the truck. The edges of her great ears flopped with every jolting step, and James felt the shock each time a foot hit the sidewalk. She raced by places he had never seen. He was sure she was going the wrong way. "Daisy?" he shouted. "Daisy!"

She stopped, but her front legs moved in place. She swung the concrete from side to side.

He patted her ears, patted the top of her head, crooned to her, "Daiiiisy. Daiiisy. Cool it. Cool it. Sloooow." At last, his voice or his words or his hands calmed her. She started back toward their part of the city.

Still, something had changed for her. Whatever Daisy knew that James didn't know about that piece of concrete made her need it badly. But the concrete didn't make her happy. Just as when James had heard Howard say Big Jim's name, finding the rubble seemed to make Daisy more upset.

After she had brought him to his window, James was glad to see her going toward the hill that led down to the zoo. It's her home, he told himself. It's her only home.

RESEARCH

A good thing about nightwalking was that James got up already dressed. There was a bad part to that, too, as he found out Thursday morning.

"Did you put your clothes in the laundry, sugar, when you took your bath?" Martha asked. "You must wear clean clothes every day."

James nodded. He sat at the kitchen table sleepily sucking milk into a straw. He put his finger over the top and moved the straw from his glass to his cereal bowl. When he lifted his finger, the milk poured out—just as the water Daisy lifted in her trunk poured down her throat.

"James, stop messing with that milk!"

He dropped the straw into his glass. Beyond Martha's scolding and his own sleepy daze, he was trying to hear the news. Bill, who was up early, had turned on the TV. Before he went to work, he liked to do his "homework," in case his taxi riders wanted to discuss the latest events. James wondered if Bill really did talk to his passengers, and if Bill would talk more to James if James gave him a tip.

The TV said nothing about a roaming elephant. James would have to get the news about Daisy for himself. She'd been so upset about the concrete, he was eager to know if she was all right, so when he left his building, he headed down the hill to the zoo. He moved cautiously, for he knew it might be even harder for a kid to walk unnoticed away from school in the morning than for an elephant to walk in city streets at night.

Menika and Beverly were standing in the elephant yard, one here, one there, dirt and bits of hay all over their backs, trunks hanging down, square as boxes. But Daisy paced fiercely near her freedom gate, swinging her piece of concrete high, low, high again, as if she were about to heave it into the distance. There were no keepers in sight.

James looked around at the moat, the bridge, the gates with their secret broken locks. He leaned over the fence and tried to make the windy, vacuuming noises Daisy made when she arrived at his window, in case they were an elephant greeting.

He was sure Daisy could hear him, but she made no sign. In a minute, when he heard a motor and the huge metal door in the stone building slid open, he thought he understood. Maybe Daisy had paid him no attention because she knew the keepers were coming out, and she didn't want them to know he was her friend. Could she be as sneaky as that?

A keeper came near where James stood, a small, slim woman who looked very strong. Her blond hair, pulled back in a ponytail, swung from side to side as she pulled a wagon carrying plastic buckets over the bumpy dirt of the yard. The keeper wore khaki shorts, heavy boots, and a sweatshirt with an elephant's head printed on the back, and ZOO STAFF and SUZY on the front. As she passed the Asian elephants, one reached a trunk toward the cart. "Menika! Leave it!" Suzy said. Menika backed away.

"Hi!" James called. "Could I ask you some questions about the African elephant? It's for a report for school."

Suzy glanced at each of the elephants and at the other keeper. "Sure." She came close to the edge of the moat.

Lying awake that morning, too worried to sleep, James had decided that something about the hunk of concrete must be familiar to Daisy, to make it so important to her. He had figured out some questions so he could learn more about her.

He asked if she was trained. Suzy told him Daisy had already liked people when she came to the zoo. She already knew her name and some commands and was learning more. Suzy held out a stick about two feet long with a metal point and a hook at one end. "Sometimes we give a little poke or pull with our commands."

James had noticed that the keepers always carried those sticks in the elephant yard. "Doesn't it hurt?" He touched the point. It wasn't sharp.

"We use the ankus as a signal, not for punishment."

Suzy talked as if she'd answered these questions a hundred times.

"How did Daisy come from Z . . . Z . . . ?" he asked.

"Zimbabwe. It's complicated. Elephants are endangered species. There are all kinds of restrictions, and not many come into the U.S. now. But they do come. We have an idea how Daisy got here. In Africa, elephants mostly live on reserves. In some countries, like Zimbabwe, the herds can grow too large for the food supply."

Menika had been coming closer, and Suzy reached up and put her hand deep into her mouth. James must have looked disgusted, for Suzy laughed. "She loves to have her tongue rubbed. She kind of sucks on our hands. We think she likes the salt on our skin." Menika looked as happy as a baby with its pacifier, but James hoped Daisy never wanted him to do that!

Suzy stopped smiling. "Anyway, when there are too many elephants and not enough food, they'll bust through the reserve fence and eat the farmers' crops. They do a lot of damage."

James remembered the mess Daisy had made breaking off branches, pulling up flowers. "Don't the farmers get mad?"

"Sure! So the government moves some elephants away, or sells some to other countries. But also"— Suzy made a face as if she didn't like what she had to say—"they kill some."

"*Kill* elephants! Just for being hungry? Just for needing food? That's horrible!"

"I hate it. But there are more and more people who have to eat, too, so there are more farms. There's pressure on both sides of the fence. Anyway, sometimes only the adult elephants are killed, and the young ones are saved to be sold. We think that's how Daisy got to this country."

"You *paid* the people who killed her family?"

"No. We wouldn't do that. We got her from a wild-animal farm. They had gotten her somewhere else, then found they couldn't afford to keep her."

"A wild-animal farm? Like a little circus!" James tried not to sound eager. "That goes around and plays in parks!"

"No. A place in Pennsylvania that rents out animals for shows and TV ads. We've been planning for an African elephant for a long time, and this farm has healthy animals."

Daisy was facing away from them now. She had put the rubble between her feet, James saw, and her trunk was up and pointed over her head toward him and Suzy. "That means Daisy's an orphan."

"I'd bet. But I think she's beginning to feel at home. We try to make the little herd here like a family. Our long-range plan is to have a real family. We'll breed Daisy, when she gets old enough.

"Elephants' families are important to them. Be sure to put that in your report. It's what I love best about them." Suzy laughed. "Their family reunions are wild! They squeal and rumble and smell each other and run around. Liquid comes streaming out of the glands on the sides of their heads and streaks down their faces."

"Would I be able hear the rumbles?" James knew he was sounding eager again.

"Maybe. They're very low, mostly infrasonic—sounds humans can't hear. I can feel them if I'm touching the elephants, or sometimes just in the air."

"Like vibrations?"

Suzy nodded. "Like the Metro."

Yes, James thought, like a Metro train coming to the station.

He watched Daisy touching the concrete all over with the tip of her trunk, sucking in its smell. The man in Big Jim's cap had said there had been a little circus in the park where she had found it. Elephants would make wonderful detectives, he thought, smelling when something's been somewhere, after it's gone. "What's she's got?" he asked Suzy.

"We don't know. We just noticed it this morning. She puts it down when she needs her trunk to eat or drink, but if we come close, she picks it right up. It looks like concrete, but we can't find the place where it broke off. She seems bothered by it. We're keeping an eye on her." Suzy waved to the other keeper. "I should go. It takes half an hour to get a snack ready for these ladies. Good luck with your report."

A few minutes after the keepers left, Daisy walked over to James, coming right to the edge of the moat.

She lifted her trunk and held her rubble out toward him. He almost could have touched it.

Parts of her face were flickering. He could sense the vibrations. She was rumbling to him, though he couldn't hear it.

He knew she needed him to do something about that concrete. Doing something, he was pretty sure, meant finding the little circus. "Okay," he told her. "I'll try."

A SOCKFUL OF SMELL

As soon as James returned to the apartment, he began his search for the little circus. The man in the cap had said it was moving to a mall, and James knew the names of the nearby malls from TV ads. After an operator helped him get the numbers, he called and kept calling. He talked to people who were rude, or bored, or who tried to be helpful but didn't know anything. He had his lunch, even though it wasn't noon yet. Then, on his next call, a man told him, yes, a little circus was set up that week in his mall's parking lot.

Before he even tried to make Daisy go someplace, James knew, he should be sure it was worth the trip. He'd have to go himself, and he really didn't want to do that. He felt shy, and sleepy, and, besides, it was almost time for *This Old World*.

After he watched the show, he set his alarm and slept for exactly an hour and a half. He woke still sleepy. He'd had two nights out with Daisy, and tonight might be another. He fixed a second lunch and wrote a note for Martha in case he was late. Then, finally, he took his red money sock and rode the Metro out to the mall.

Bright posters, high flags, and band music led him across the parking lot to the circus. People, mostly school groups, were coming out of a blue, green, and white-striped tent. James held a tent flap open and, since no one even looked at him, he went inside.

A man in a suit and tall hat of shiny blue was waving a sparkly wand in time to the music. He signaled to a clown who was sitting at a board full of switches beside the ring. The music stopped and the lights went off, leaving only gray light seeping in as the last people left.

Outside again, James saw no sign of animals, though he smelled an animal smell. Wandering, he found the ringmaster, now dressed in jeans and a red shirt, carrying a rake. His short dark beard, which had looked elegant with his fancy blue suit, now made him look tough. Before James could say anything, the man pointed. "The ticket office is over there."

The office was four wide boards standing on end on a little platform, making a square room just large enough to hold a tiny table and chair. A woman in shiny-blue pants and shirt lay back in the chair, her eyes closed. James watched her through the window. After a moment she sat up, unlocked a drawer in the table, pulled out a thermos and brown bag, and began to eat a sandwich.

James stepped close. The woman glanced at him

and took another bite. She had long curly dark hair and lots of makeup. A seam of her blue shirt had been mended with red thread. To James, she looked exactly as a circus lady should. "Hello," he said.

She took a long drink, then smiled a welcoming smile. "Hi."

James felt awkward asking about elephants right off. Anyway, the smell Daisy cared about might not even be an elephant's. But how could *he* recognize the smell *she* knew? Suppose Daisy was madly in love with a trained seal? Or a chimpanzee? Suppose she had plans for a terrible revenge on a chimp who once stole her banana? Suppose . . . ? Suppose! He couldn't believe he was so stupid an elephant had made him come all the way out here to talk to . . .

"We're sold out tomorrow and Saturday," the woman said. "We have a few seats left for Sunday. Our last day."

"You're leaving? Are you going far?"

"Two P.M. show Wednesday in Cincinnati. We have to leave at dawn Monday. Come Sunday! It's a nice show. You like monkeys? We have some great little fellows—they ride tricycles, they play instruments. We train our animals well."

"How much are the tickets?"

"Twelve dollars. Noon show or three o'clock? And how many?"

Twelve dollars! He wouldn't give so much, unless . . . "Do you have an elephant? Did you used to?"

"Oh, we have an elephant now!" The woman laughed. "But our baby's *not* so well trained. She's smart, she'll learn. Pumpkin's a sweetie."

"Pumpkin!" What a stupid name!

"We got her on Halloween."

Pumpkin! Still, it was an elephant. Slowly James pulled his sock from his pocket, trying to calculate how little he'd have left. "One ticket," he said. "For three o'clock."

"Oh, get two! A circus is much more fun with a friend! Nobody goes to the circus alone!"

James couldn't tell if this woman's smile was friendly or mean. He didn't want her to be suspicious that he was here to check out her elephant. Through the sock he felt the hard curves and crackles of his money. But he couldn't keep saving for an emergency his whole life: Sometimes an emergency comes. Daisy's emergency was right now. "Okay. Two."

"Twenty-five forty-four with the tax," the woman said.

James pushed some bills through the window. The woman pushed back some change and two large green tickets, decorated with gold flourishes and musical notes. If no one came with him Sunday, James thought, he would save the other beautiful ticket forever.

The woman locked most of his fortune away in a metal box. "See you Sunday!" She snatched another bite of her sandwich.

James took a chance. "I'm doing a report on ele-phants for school. Can you tell me about . . ." He couldn't say that stupid name. ". . . your elephant? Is she African or Asian? And how she got here, and how old she is?"

"We don't know much about Pumpkin. Our supplier thinks she's not even two yet. She's from Africa. Zimbabwe."

"Zimbabwe!"

"Yes. The supplier had just gotten them in. We take the little ones and only keep them about a year. We'll train her good, then sell her to a zoo. The supplier said Pumpkin and her. . . ."

A loud whistle, like a police whistle, cut her off. James wished the woman would finish her sentence. *What?* he wanted to scream. Pumpkin and her *what?*

But the woman was swearing, wrapping up the rest of her sandwich, standing up. "My husband needs some help. But I get so hungry!" She smiled. "Come on. He doesn't like people back there while the animals rest after the show, but maybe you can see her."

See her! Forget about Daisy's mission; James was thrilled to see *any* baby elephant!

Following the woman around the tent, he saw stilts and colored balls, three small tricycles and a wagon resting by an entrance. Buckets were stacked near two big barrels, and sparrows pecked at the ground nearby, picking up grain that had spilled.

They came to three trucks decorated with huge pictures of a giraffe, a tiger, a gorilla. Each truck had one side folded up, revealing a wall of bars. The animals inside, eating or resting, were not so wild as the ones painted on the outside. Two trucks had several cages—monkeys and some dogs were in one truck, a pony and two parrots in another. The elephant had a truck to herself.

James stopped cold when he saw her, a creature at once so tiny and cute, and so large! She was as tall as the pony and much fatter, yet she looked like a baby. Just one of her ears, folded back against her head, was bigger than her whole face. Her slim, lively trunk was flipping around, picking apples from the floor and putting them in her mouth.

Her cage was small. The ringmaster had to bend over inside, raking her straw.

"Did you feed the little fellows yet?" the woman asked. The man shook his head. "I'll go," she said. "Ed's working on that engine. This kid's doing a report on elephants. He wants to look at Pumpkin. Okay?" She left, and James was sorry. He guessed the man wouldn't be so friendly. He seemed like the owner, the boss.

The man's eyes flickered toward him for a second. "Go ahead. Look." He turned his back and went on raking.

James looked. The baby elephant stomped a foot, lifted her tail up over her back, and flapped one ear forward. She put an apple in her mouth, then swung the end of her trunk up into her ear and left it there while she chewed. This baby looked as if she could be part of Daisy's family, James thought. But as far as he knew, so did every elephant in Africa.

As he took a step closer, the baby elephant turned slightly. Suddenly her trunk shot out between the bars, straight toward him, and he heard the windy, vacuuming sound.

He glanced toward the man. He was raking the far end of the truck now. He didn't notice the vibrations throbbing on the little elephant's forehead or see how intensely she was smelling the sleeve of James's sweatshirt.

James brought his arm up to his nose. He couldn't smell anything. But these were the clothes he'd worn the night before: He must smell of Daisy! The smell told the baby the news.

From the back of the cage came the sound of squeaking metal. The man had opened a door on the truck's far side and was shoving out the dirty hay. He jumped down and slammed the door.

James had only a moment to do whatever he would do. He yanked his sock from his pocket and held it out for the baby elephant to touch. He rubbed it against her trunk.

"Hey! Get away from her!" The man had come around the truck. "Back off! Back off!" He whacked the bars with his rake. The baby squealed and pulled her trunk inside.

James pushed the sock deep into his pocket. "I'm sorry," he said. "I . . ."

"Step back!" The man leapt up behind the truck's cab and unfastened a rope. He gave it a jerk and the side of the truck unfolded its many little folds, slithering down over the bars to make a wall. As he left, James heard thumping behind him and a frightened yelp.

At the edge of the grass, he picked up a plastic bag and tightly wrapped the red sock loaded with the smell of a baby elephant.

A TRIP TO THE CIRCUS

James came in just as Martha was rewinding the VCR tape with the day's stories. She smiled to him. "I was just fixing to worry about you, sugar. Go on and get your tray. I'll wait."

Later, in the kitchen during *This Old World*, James studied Bill's map and located the mall, north of the city. He was glad to see that Rock Creek, which they had followed to the zoo the first night, continued straight north. He knew he'd been lucky not to be caught so far, but late at night there would be few cars on the road by the creek. They should be able to get to the mall safely—*if* he could get Daisy to go where he wanted. He never had.

He would need something to signal her with, something like the ankus Suzy had showed him. As quietly as possible, he searched the kitchen drawers. A hammer, he decided, would work best. He could gently poke Daisy in the right direction with the claw. With the hammer hidden under his shirt, James went straight to his room.

He took his bath quickly. He was so tired that as soon as he had wrapped his things in his sweatshirt and called good-night to Martha, he put his pillow on the floor by the window. He would have to count on Daisy to wake him tonight.

As he dozed off, he imagined what might happen if the two elephants met. He hoped they wouldn't tear the place apart, but he had to risk it. Daisy needed to see that little elephant.

He woke at one thirty, with Daisy's trunk-fingers snuffling in his ear. He grabbed his sweatshirt bundle and climbed outside. He could tell that Daisy was still upset, though she hadn't brought the rubble with her. Without stopping once at a corner, she headed back toward the little park where she had found it.

James leaned down. "Daisy!" Her ear twitched, but she kept going. "Daisy!" He touched her neck with the claw of the hammer, pressing in the direction he needed her to go. She slowed just a little. James didn't know if he was giving a signal she understood. Keeping the hammer's pressure on her neck, he leaned to the side and held out an arm, pointing. "Daisy! Left!"

She stopped. Her trunk curved up and felt his arm and his pointing hand, then his other hand and the hammer. Then she began to walk again, in the same direction she'd been going. What an impossible elephant! She had practically begged James to help her find that baby elephant, and now that he had, she wouldn't listen to him!

He had brought the red sock with him, but Daisy had been so excited since she found the concrete, he was reluctant to use it. Now there seemed no other way to move her thousands of pounds in the direction she must go. James unfolded his sweatshirt and pulled out the plastic bag.

He had barely opened it before her trunk was up, feeling the bag, grabbing the sock from him. Luckily he had taken out his money and his paper of phone numbers. She whipped her trunk down, then high, flailing the air. She slapped the sock against her cheek, then put it in her mouth and held it there, still as still, as if she were breathing the little elephant into her.

James pressed the hammer into her neck. "Daisy! Go!" This time her head, then her feet turned the way he needed her to go. Daisy was off, with an eager high marching step James had never seen her use before. She held the red sock high in an S salute, a flag leading her parade.

They went back down the hill toward the zoo. When they came to the creek, James said, "Daisy! Right!" and signaled with the hammer. She moved into the water and splashed northward through the dark woods.

Rock Creek twisted and curved along, a perfect hidden highway. Daisy didn't seem to mind the many rocks and boulders in the shallow parts. Where the creek ran deep, she half floated, her feet pushing lightly against the bottom. If a bridge was too low or a waterfall too high, she got out and walked around it. When she came to a tree fallen across the creek, she simply pushed it out of her way.

When the woods thinned out and the creek became small, they moved out onto curved streets where houses were far apart, onto broad streets with large buildings. Whenever James, following the map he had drawn, gave a signal to turn, Daisy obeyed without breaking stride.

Just as he caught sight of the Metro entrance near the mall, though, Daisy stopped. She lifted her trunk and ears as if she was receiving new signals, then started on even faster. Her tail curled up over her back in a knot of excitement. She seemed to know exactly where she was going now, and James was certain she knew who she would find.

When they came to the mall's vast, empty parking lot, James called, "Daisy! Slow!" He pressed the hammer claw against her forehead, pulling back as a horse rider would pull on the reins.

Daisy didn't slow. She ran to the grassy area where light from the parking-lot lamps spilled onto the circus park. She ran to the largest truck, squealing now, the way Yolanda used to squeal and giggle when her cousin came in the door. The side of the truck was down, but James could hear answering squeals through a small, high window.

Daisy slapped her ears against her sides. Her tusks clacked against the window bars. Soon she was dancing, dancing for joy, James thought. He held tight to her ears so as not to fall under her busy, heavy feet. The air seemed full of vibrations. In another truck, a dog began to bark.

A small trunk appeared between the window bars, just a few inches of it, but as mysterious and thrilling as the large trunk first coming through James's window two nights before. The little trunk strained toward the big one, strained like a baby holding out its arms, wanting to be picked up, wanting more.

Daisy stopped dancing. Her trunk grabbed the baby's, hugging it, the two trunks slithering up and down each other, flipping and twitching, knotting and unknotting. Before Daisy could begin stomping again, James slid off and backed away.

The vibrations in the air grew stronger, like a rush hour's worth of Metro trains. These elephants must know each other, James thought. The little one must be Daisy's sister, or her cousin, or her niece.

Daisy wrapped her trunk around a window bar, testing it as if she meant to tear the truck apart. James wondered if he should try to stop her. He wondered if he could.

She spread her ears to the fullest and raised her head. This time when Daisy trumpeted, the noise was so close James's ears felt stunned, as if the shriek had smacked him. When it was over, the yapping of little dogs, the pony's neigh, the monkeys' frightened chatter, seeped slowly into the silence.

Daisy swung her heavy foot against a tire, then pressed a tusk into it. That corner of the truck sank slightly. She went behind the truck and placed her forehead against it. The sounds from the other animals grew louder, and James was afraid the circus people might wake up. "Daisy!" he said urgently. "Daisy!"

She pushed as if she couldn't hear him, or didn't care. The truck moved slightly. She backed off as if she meant to ram it.

Then, from the far side of the truck, came a crack like gunfire.

The baby elephant shrieked, the dogs barked furiously. Daisy jerked upright and bolted away. With her trunk flailing the air, and all the while looking behind her, she ran halfway across the parking lot. James raced after her, but she took no notice of him and came circling back toward the truck.

There was another sharp crack, and a shout. "Pumpkin!"

James had followed Daisy back toward the truck, waving his arms above his head. This time as she bolted away, she saw him. She helped him onto her back, then turned and stared behind her, raising one foot then the other.

The circus owner had come from behind the truck, wearing his high boots over his pajamas. His long hair sprang wildly in all directions. He looked at the tire Daisy had damaged, then he shouted angrily and smashed his fist against the truck. *Bang!*

The baby elephant squealed, Daisy trumpeted, and the man turned around. His mouth opened slowly but no words came out. In the other trucks, the animals howled and screamed.

James lay low, glad he had worn dark clothes, holding tight to Daisy's ears and peeking over her forehead. He could imagine Daisy as the man saw her: a huge, gray giant, wild and threatening, who couldn't possibly be there, under the parking-lot lights of a suburban mall.

Slowly, the man came toward her, shouting, and smashing his fist against one truck, then another. *Bang! Bang! Bang!*

Daisy ran again, leaving now for sure, James thought as he pressed himself against her back. Perhaps she remembered the sound of gunshots, from when hunters killed her family.

Had these two elephants last seen each other months ago, when people shot the adults of their family and took them away to sell? Had they last seen each other at the animal-supply place when one of them was sold away? James knew he was making up stories about them. He would never know their real stories, or even whether their stories were the same story. All of that was inside their long elephant memories, unavailable to words.

The man soon gave up chasing Daisy. Looking back, James saw him holding his fist high, like a threat.

As if in answer as she ran, Daisy held high the red sock, like a promise she would return.

Going back through the creek, she splashed through the water furiously, not being careful at all and soaking James. There was no way he could calm her. Just once, standing in water up to her belly, she turned and looked behind her. "Daisy!" he said softly. "No. Not yet." He didn't know whether she heard, or understood, but she kept on going downstream.

James was exhausted. He put his head down, but his mind raced. He was thrilled that he had helped Daisy find the little elephant who meant so much to her. He had never made anything so important happen before. But he was also frightened, for he knew this was not the end of the help Daisy needed. This was just the beginning.

LOCKED GATES

Later that morning, Friday morning, lying in bed afraid to sleep for fear he wouldn't be able to get up, James worried about Daisy. He decided he must go to the zoo again, instead of going to school. First, as soon as Martha left, he took his wet clothes from where he'd hidden them wrapped in a towel under his bed and dried them in the basement laundry room. The dryer cost $1.50. Hanging out with Daisy was really expensive!

He found the huge metal door from the elephant house to the yard open only far enough for a human to get by. Through the crack, James could see Daisy inside, pacing back and forth. He heard a slamming noise each time she turned.

He also heard the *chink, chink,* of metal striking metal. A man was working at one of the gates to the bridge over the dry moat. Suzy was standing by him. James moved closer and called, "Hi!" When she waved, he asked what they were doing.

"Something weird happened." She said the owner of

a small circus had called and complained that an elephant had been there the night before, making a ruckus and upsetting his animals. "I told him all our elephants were right here, secure. Then I walked the fence and found the locks broken—on both gates! We're fixing the locks—and putting in an electric fence, next week. We don't know what could have happened."

"What did the elephant do out there?" James asked carefully.

"All the guy actually said was it gave his truck a flat tire! That doesn't make sense. He must have had a nightmare." The repairman called Suzy over to answer a question, and afterward she seemed to forget about James, walking away along the moat, kicking stones.

James followed her, opening the notebook he had brought as an excuse for asking questions. "Maybe the elephant who was at the circus was looking for its family."

Suzy looked up startled, as if she had forgotten he was there.

"Those circuses that come around sometimes have elephants," he said. "Maybe she wanted to see another elephant." He hoped that idea would interest Suzy, but she just looked confused. "Remember, you told me elephants love their families? Maybe her family's there."

"Look, I'm not even sure I believe there was an elephant out there." Suzy shrugged. "Shouldn't you be in school?"

"Well. You know. I'm doing this report."

Suzy put her foot on a stump and stared at him, really looked at him for the first time. "I never saw you before, now you're here all the time. Did your family just move here?"

"*I* just moved here. To my new family."

Suzy looked puzzled, but James didn't help her. He had been through this conversation many times. He knew where it was going, and he hated it. When she thought she had the answer, Suzy asked, "Did you just get adopted?"

"I live with a foster family."

"Oh. Oh! I always wondered about that. So, do you like your new family?"

"They're okay. I liked the one I had before better, but I couldn't stay."

"That's tough," Suzy said. The man had finished fixing the locks. "That must be really hard." Suzy kept looking at James as if she was trying to understand how it would feel to move into a new home, away from the family you knew. But the man was waiting, and she waved and went inside.

Soon James heard an electric hum as the big door opened. He moved downwind so Daisy wouldn't smell him. He had learned that much about elephants.

As soon as she could fit through the door's opening, Daisy trotted out. She was holding the red sock. James saw that she was just as she'd been the night before, tense and angry. The Asian elephants ambled out to begin their dust bath, and the keepers stood in the door, talking and watching, mostly watching Daisy. She rubbed the sock against her leg, against her cheek, against her ear. Every now and then she shook her head sharply, and her ears snapped.

James remembered how eagerly she had run in the streets, searching for that baby; how she had challenged George Washington's statue horse; how she had loved picking her own snacks from the trees. Now all her playfulness, all her confidence, all her calm purpose, was gone. She looked so frantic, so miserable, he couldn't bear to watch. He turned away and left.

As he came onto his block, James saw Karen Grande going toward his building. He ducked into a doorway, but she had seen him.

"What's up, James?" Karen put her hand on his shoulder and led him to the steps of his apartment house. They sat on the warm stone in the warm spring sunshine, but James did not feel at all comfortable.

"Emergency visit," Karen said. "The school called Martha, and she called me. She said you've been very quiet. She thought . . . something might have happened. But you don't look like an emergency, you look sad. Trouble at school?"

"School's okay. I'm worried about an elephant."

"An elephant!"

James nodded. "One of the elephants down at the zoo is really unhappy. Her sister or her cousin or somebody is in a circus, and they're *both* unhappy, because, you know . . . they want to be together."

Above her gay red blouse, Karen's serious eyes stared at him long and hard. "Are *you* unhappy, James, with Bill and Martha?"

"*Me?* Well, I don't like it as much as with Big Jim."

"James? Do yourself a favor. Forget about Big Jim. I know it's tough, moving to a new place, but it's better than the group home, isn't it?" He nodded. "Is the food okay?"

"The food's good."

"And Martha and Bill?"

"They're pretty tired. She wants me to give him a Father's Day present. Do I have to?"

"It might be nice. But it's weeks till Father's Day— why don't you wait and see how you feel then? James? People are often uncomfortable in a new placement, until everyone gets used to each other. Give it a chance."

"Anyway, what I'm worried about is the elephant. You should see her, slamming around, swinging her trunk, banging things."

"That's really sad, if . . . How do you know so much about this elephant?"

Even with Karen, he couldn't tell it all. If she took him away because Daisy could find him at Bill and Martha's, he might never see Daisy again. "I'm writing a report for school." And, he thought, I've already found out enough for college.

"Will you read some to me?" Karen asked.

"Sure. This is just from my research. This part's due Monday." He opened his notebook. " 'Elephants are social animals. They go in groups. Their main group is their family. The adult males leave, but the rest stay with their families their whole life. The sisters and aunts and mothers and grandmothers and all the kids and cousins play together.

" 'Each family has an old, important mother who remembers how to do things and decides where they eat and when they're going to sleep or have a bath. The big kids sit the babies, just like for people.' "

Maybe Daisy was that baby's sitter, he thought as he turned the page.

" 'Lions in Africa and tigers in Asia attack the babies, but the only enemy for adult elephants is humans. So elephants are very peaceful.' That's all, but I still have to do more."

"That's really interesting," Karen said. "I hope you'll let me read it when it's done."

"The elephant at the zoo isn't peaceful," James said. "I tried to tell the keeper those elephants need each other. She wasn't very interested."

"The elephant wasn't interested?"

"The keeper."

"The elephant keeper's a woman?" Karen gave a huge smile.

James couldn't believe how much that stuff meant to Karen. "An elephant wouldn't care if the keeper's a man or a woman," he told her. "The only difference between them is like forty pounds, and an elephant weighs maybe four tons. Why would an elephant care?" He waited to see if she was ready to get back to what was important: "So how could I help those elephants?"

"Help an elephant family?" Karen shook her head so fast her curly black hair flipped all around. "I can't even help human families as much as I'd like! Speaking of which, I have to go, and *you* have to go to school."

"Do I have to? Probably it's past recess. Almost lunch!"

Karen looked at her watch.

"Friday afternoon isn't much. Just music. Then conflict resolution." He watched her face to see how he was doing. "I don't get in many conflicts." She was smiling now. "Then she reads to us, and I already read that book. Please? I promise I'll work on my report. Please?"

"Well. I'll call Martha and Ms. Jackson and tell them you're home working on your report, and that you'll be in school Monday. Monday you *must* go to school. And give Martha and Bill a chance. If you have a problem, try talking about it with them."

"My problem," James said, "is the elephant."

Karen hoisted her sack onto her shoulder. "James? Really. Work on your report. You seem to have a nice feeling for elephants. Okay?"

"Okay," he said softly. "Thank you." Thank you for

my afternoon, he thought as he watched her hurry to her car, but I wish you'd help me help Daisy.

He sat on the stoop, trying to figure out what to do. Karen wouldn't help him. Suzy didn't even seem curious about the circus elephant—though to be fair, he hadn't told either one all that he knew. He was used to people not understanding. In every home he'd been in—even with Big Jim—he'd understood things, had known about things, the grown-ups had not.

Who could he ask to help? He didn't know many people. He had a flicker of an idea, but he quickly put it away. Big Jim hadn't come to the home to see him, and James couldn't bear to hear Big Jim say no to him about this. He shook his head hard, like an elephant snapping her ears, and walked slowly back to the zoo. He had no reason. He had no plan. He just wanted to be near Daisy.

Long before he got close to the elephant house, he saw the red sock waving. Daisy was by the gate, turning away, turning back, swinging her trunk toward the lock, then away again. Two keepers he didn't know and a man in a suit were outside the fence, watching her.

Watching them, James came closer than he meant to, and the next time Daisy turned, she noticed him. She stopped pacing and put out her ears and trunk. The keepers and the man in the suit stopped talking.

Quickly, James turned toward Menika, who was

leaning against a tree with her rear legs crossed. When one of the keepers called "Daisy!," Daisy went to the back of the yard. Soon the people were talking again.

Daisy tossed her head and gave the whole front of her body a mighty shake. Her ears smacked her shoulders, and a *whoosh* of air shot from her trunk. She wasn't pretending any longer. Her ears, her trunk, and her body were aimed straight at James.

There was no sense in him pretending, either. He moved toward her along the fence, knowing the others were watching. As Daisy came to meet him, he felt a great burst of love. He had missed her terribly, knowing she was locked up now, knowing there would be no nightwalk tonight.

When she was as close to him as she could get, with just the fence and the moat between them, Daisy stretched out her trunk. The red sock hung in the air between them.

"I know," James said. "I will."

As the keepers and the man in the suit hurried over, Daisy went to the back of the yard, leaving James to do whatever he could on the humans' side of the fence.

"I'd keep away from that elephant," one keeper warned him. "She's uneasy today."

"Does she know you?" the man asked. "She seems to know you."

"I come here a lot," James said. "I'm doing a

report." He was glad Suzy wasn't there to hear that dumb excuse again.

"You don't feed her, do you?" the man asked.

"No! I never give her anything to eat."

"Well, be careful!" the other keeper said. "Wild animals can be dangerous. Seeing you seemed to bother her. You'd better stay away for a few days."

Glad to be let off so easily, James hurried away. Going up the hill, though, he almost came to a stop. Whether or not Daisy had understood his words, he had made her another promise. But what could he do? What could a kid really do?

Maybe Big Jim could do something. He was good at doing. Even if James wasn't brave enough to call Big Jim for himself, maybe he could call Big Jim for Daisy.

HANZVADZI

On Saturday, after Martha finally got James up, they went to buy him clothes at her department store. She also bought a shirt for him to give Bill on Father's Day. The store was big and neat and full of clean, folded, brand-new clothes, but the whole trip took three and a half hours, and they did not have lunch out.

As soon as he'd had something to eat, James laid his new clothes out on his bed. He had two pairs of pants, two pairs of jeans, two long-sleeved shirts, four T-shirts, four sets of underwear and socks. The T-shirts were especially nice—Martha had let him choose those himself.

As he put the clothes away, he noticed the blue sock where he kept his money now. Once again, he counted what was left. It was pitiful. He had to remind himself that the circus woman might not have talked to him so much, might not have let him meet the baby elephant, if he hadn't bought the tickets. Those tickets were like a present to Daisy.

He should go to the circus tomorrow, he thought,

to learn whatever he could learn, before he did whatever he could do. Whatever he did, he had to do it before the circus left, at dawn Monday.

Probably Karen would like him to invite Martha or Bill to go with him. But Martha could go out a whole morning and not buy even one snack, and he didn't know Bill that well.

He could invite Big Jim to go with him, to show him the baby elephant before he asked him to help. He had thought it would be easy to call Big Jim if he was doing it for Daisy, but he hadn't called.

He put some money and the paper with Mama's phone number and his library card into his pocket and went out. When he came to a pay phone, he looked at Mama's number, then he walked right on to the Metro station.

He was going to the main library, for he wanted to get not only some of his favorite storybooks, but a Zimbabwe word that would be a better name for the little elephant called Pumpkin. "Could you find the word for sister?" he asked a librarian. Daisy would like that, he thought, if she could understand. The librarian looked in some books and called someone and told James that the main language in Zimbabwe is Chishona, and that the Chishona word for sister is *hanzvadzi*. They practiced saying it, and James wrote it down.

On his way back, he did stop at the pay phone. Mama answered. James whispered, "Hello," and her warm voice bounded back to him: "Is that you, James?"

He swallowed and remembered Big Jim's rule: *Never try to fool Mama—Mama always knows.* "Yes. Hello, Mama."

"Why, hello, James!" Mama talked awhile, without James saying much. She asked him about school, and invited him to come have supper one evening, and told him news about the boy who lived next door. "I'll get Big Jim," she said at last. "But don't you go tearing up his heart." James heard the phone clatter onto the table by the stairs in Mama's front hall.

He remembered how that big boy next door and his big friends used to tease him when he visited Mama, until one evening Big Jim went out to talk to them. James had stayed in that dark hall, scrunched up under that little table, listening while the noise of their rough play suddenly went quiet, listening to the softness of Big Jim's voice. Then Big Jim came in and hugged James. He said only, "Well, we had a little conversation"; but after that, whenever James visited, that boy and James were friends.

He heard the phone being picked up. He felt Big Jim's high, happy voice wrap around him, blocking out everything else in the world. "How you doin', James?"

"Good. How you doin', Big Jim?" James knew exactly what the answer would be.

"About half. No, I'd say three quarters, now *you*

called. They treating you all right? You eating good?"
Right away they were talking as if they had seen each
other just last week.

"*I'm* eating fine. How about *you*? I heard you
moved to Mama's."

"Just because I live here doesn't mean I have to eat
here! You being good? You going to school?"

James hesitated for a second. "Mostly."

"I don't want to hear 'mostly.' You *go* to school!"

"Okay, Big Jim. Big Jim, I got tickets to a circus. You
want to go to the circus with me tomorrow?"

"Tomorrow? The circus? Is it my birthday or something, you inviting me to go to a circus?"

"Nobody's birthday. Just . . . tomorrow's when I got
tickets for." Or maybe, he thought, because Father's
Day's going to be coming. Father's Day, Father's Day!
James chanted to himself. Maybe that's why I'm
inviting you—and because I need you tomorrow. "Can
you come?"

"I'll be there. Where do I have to be?"

The next afternoon, right after dinner, which was
right after church, James told Martha he was meeting
a friend to go to a show. Though it was a bright spring
day with just the slightest breeze, he put on his winter
jacket. He took his mittens and scarf with him, too,
and one of Bill's big caps, all stuffed into his pockets.
To hide from the circus people's eyes and the baby
elephant's nose, he needed a good disguise.

On the Metro platform, Big Jim looked just great, just the same. He wore a lavender shirt and the black-leather vest James admired so much. He was a small man and slim, but he was strong, James knew, from being a carpenter. James used to love to feel the muscles in his arms. Big Jim was moving around, looking around, restless, until he saw James walking toward him. Then he stood still and grinned.

As they talked, James glanced down every few minutes to enjoy the shine on Big Jim's high-heeled boots. He watched Big Jim's quick eyes checking out whether the train was coming. "You got new shaving foam!" he said. "You didn't tell me."

"James, you always did have a nose like a dog. You like it?"

"Yeah, but . . ." Well, a man had a right to change his shaving foam! James just wished he'd known. All these days he'd been smelling the wrong one. "Yeah, it's *fine!*"

Big Jim was checking out James, too. "Why're you wearing that big, heavy coat?" he asked. "Don't your new people have any heat?" James smiled, but he didn't answer. They stepped onto the train and, for the fun of it, stood all the way.

Though they arrived early enough to sit up front in the tent, James asked to sit in back. With just three tiers of seats in the tent, everybody could see well, and it was safer that way.

Big Jim said later he had had no idea such a little

circus could give you such a great big time. There was music, and colored lights, and the animals wore costumes. The owner, dressed in his shiny blue, cracked his whip every few minutes and waved his sparkly wand.

Each act had one or two animals. A dog pulled a tiny wagon with a monkey hopping in and out, doing tricks. The monkeys, dressed like ballerinas, waved flags and played on drums. The circus woman tap-danced—once with a monkey for her partner. The clown did some silly stuff, and later he juggled balls and bowling pins.

James's favorite act was a parrot riding the pony. The pony with plumes on its head and ribbons on its tail carried a perch for the parrot to stand on. The parrot hollered, "Go right! Go left! Slow down, you fool!" James was amazed that a pony could understand a parrot, until Big Jim showed him how the circus owner was signaling to the pony with his whip.

Between acts, James looked at his paper and practiced saying *hanzvadzi*. The librarian had told him the word meant not only sister, but brother and cousin, too. She said in Zimbabwe the uncles and aunts and parents and grandparents live close together and the kids all run around together in one big family. The name was perfect for this baby elephant, James thought. He felt sure she was part of Daisy's family—though what part, he didn't know.

He didn't see Hanzvadzi for a long time. Finally, the

ringmaster picked up an ankus and shouted, "And now! Coming Attractions!" The circus woman led in the baby elephant, who had a round, orange cap sitting crooked on her head. The man led her to the center of the ring, and as he talked, she walked here and there on a long lead. James slipped on his mittens and Bill's cap.

"Pumpkin doesn't know many tricks yet," the owner told the crowd. "But elephants are among the smartest animals on earth. This baby has already taught me a few things!" The audience laughed. "We work together every day. If you'll mark your calendars to come back this fall, I think she'll surprise you."

Hanzvadzi was walking just inside the ring, a wooden circle a foot high and a foot wide. She stretched her thin trunk toward the popcorn bags and soda cups on the ground, though she couldn't reach them. When she came to the section where James sat, she curved her trunk high in an S salute. "Ooooo!" the audience murmured. She looked cute, but James knew she was smelling hard.

The owner also knew. Still talking smoothly, he moved toward her, tightening the line as he came. Hanzvadzi climbed up onto the ring, and when he pulled on her line, she didn't budge. Her trunk, straight out now and almost touching people in the front row, was pointed straight at James. Even Big Jim could tell: "Something's wrong with that thing!"

James wondered if he smelled of Daisy. He hadn't

been close to her since Thursday night. He'd had two baths since, plus he had on all these clothes. Or maybe Hanzvadzi recognized *his* smell. Did his own smell mean something to her now?

James was worried: If Hanzvadzi tried to get to him, she could hurt the people in her way. He dropped his program on the floor, and when he knelt to get it, he wrapped his scarf around his face just below his eyes. Maybe that would hold in the smell of his breath.

The man had stepped between Hanzvadzi and the audience. Some people in front had begun to leave. "Let's go!" James moved with the crowd toward the nearest tent flap, keeping Big Jim between himself and the ring.

"It's all right, ladies and gentlemen, boys and girls," the ringmaster called. "Sometimes Pumpkin gets a little curious, like any baby." He took his ankus from under his arm. James didn't see what he did with it, but he heard Hanzvadzi squeal.

As the owner hurried her to the far exit, he signaled to the clown at the control board. "We'll see you this fall!" he shouted over the swelling music. "With a better-behaved little elephant. Boys and girls! You be good too, so your parents will bring you back! Have a fantabulous summer!" The owner bowed, and prodded Hanzvadzi out of the tent.

James felt terrible leaving her, but there was nothing he could do. Yet, he told himself as he walked out. There was nothing he could do, yet.

Outside, Big Jim looked at James, then at the bright-blue sky. "You think snow's likely?" James didn't explain, but he unwrapped his scarf, unzipped his jacket, and took off his mittens and the cap. Too late, he noticed the circus woman by the little ticket house calling good-bye to the audience. When she waved a friendly wave to James, he had to wave back.

Big Jim had a way of slipping smoothly through a crowd. To keep close, James pressed his hand against the sleek leather vest. Soon Big Jim dropped his arm across James's shoulder. As they walked along, talking and not talking, James felt safe and calm and sure, the way he always had with Big Jim, the way he did riding Daisy.

Then he remembered: He still hadn't told Big Jim about Daisy.

A YOU-AND-ME SITUATION

Just as James had hoped, Big Jim turned in at a fast-food place. They each got fries, cheeseburgers, milk shakes, and pies. "Feels like home to you and me," Big Jim said as they settled into a booth. James nodded. His mouth was already full.

"I have to eat out all the time now." Big Jim was unwrapping his food, arranging it on his tray. "Even crackers from a box taste musty in Mama's kitchen. I don't know what that woman's problem is. Big pots of greasy soup in the fridge. Always trying to get me to eat her biscuits, hard as rocks. It's a wonder she raised me to where I knew what good food was and could start going out to get me some. But she is family. She's the only one I've got to tease me now."

James enjoyed this grumbling. He knew Big Jim loved Mama. "I could stand to live there," he mumbled around his straw. Right away, he held his breath. How had he dared say that!

Now it was Big Jim who took a bite so big he couldn't talk. When he spoke at last, his voice was low.

"I asked, James. After I moved. I've still got my good job, so I called Ms. Karen Grande. She said it didn't fit the guidelines, my home. She said it was not stable enough. Not a suitable home. I had. She said." He took another bite, and James could hardly understand the rest of the words popping out of his mouth. " 'Love and let go.' She said. Not 'fit.' Social-work talk!"

While Big Jim finished off his sandwich, chewing and drinking and getting his voice clear, James nibbled at a fry and kept his eyes down.

Finally, Big Jim said, "The food's not suitable, I know that!"

They laughed so loud, then, so loud, so long, so high and low, other people in the restaurant looked at them and looked away and looked again.

"Then what?" James asked, when they were quiet. "Then what, after Karen said that?"

"Then?" Big Jim asked. "Then I didn't see anything I could do."

"Well, what if . . . ?" James began, but he didn't know what to ask, or what to hope for as an answer. "Is that why you didn't come see me at the home?"

"It wouldn't do us any good," Big Jim said, "you or me either, me coming to see you when I'd just have to go away again. It didn't seem like we had any business to keep knowing each other's lives. I just couldn't come, James."

"But then at least I would know. . . ." He couldn't say how much he had needed him, with Big Jim looking so sad, so he asked, "Did you find out about Yolanda?"

Big Jim shook his head to show that what he had found out was bad news. "I don't think she'll be coming back." They were quiet a long time, each searching through the papers on his tray for a last small crunchy fry.

After a while, James said, "I wish I could get her."

"Yolanda? Who? Karen Grande?"

"Noooo, Big Jim!" James said. "That little elephant."

"What you want with an elephant?"

How much should James tell? He'd been waiting and waiting, and now, with Big Jim right here asking, he wasn't sure what to say. Big Jim was always on him not to miss a day of school, always to get a good night's sleep: "You got to be bright-eyed in the morning, sharp and ready when the teacher calls on you." Big Jim would not like what James had been doing.

Still, he had promised Daisy. "Can I tell you something?"

"You can tell me anything you like, after I get me a cup of coffee. You want another pie?"

"Cherry, please." James watched Big Jim getting impatient in the line, waving back to him, jiggling his knees, flirting with the woman behind the counter, making her laugh.

When he came back, he let James fix his coffee: two sugars, four creams. "Now tell me."

"You remember," James began, "when I needed to change my class you got me in Ms. McKenna's?"

"That other teacher was a mess."

"Ms. McKenna really liked me. You got me in her class."

"I did?"

"You remember!"

"Now, how did I do that?"

"*I* don't know! *You're* the one who did it! Talking, I guess." James was standing now, standing right up in the booth to stop Big Jim's teasing, grinning and trying not to grin, for he was scared now. He badly needed Big Jim to remember about his life. "You remember! You went over there, and when you came home you said I was in Ms. McKenna's."

Big Jim nodded. "I remember we had a little conversation."

"That was the best thing . . . ! And now . . . it's the same. To make a change because . . . something's wrong. Those two elephants want to be with each other. Will you talk to the keeper?"

"Who, two elephants? I don't know what you're talking about, James."

"That elephant we saw at the circus. . . . Well, there's another elephant I know. . . . See, I'm doing a report. Big Jim, can I say it, and you won't get mad? I missed some school."

"I'm not going to get mad, James."

Still, James couldn't tell about riding out on Daisy. The rest of the story he told Big Jim was amazing enough—the elephants smelling each other on him and going wild—and confusing enough that Big Jim didn't ask uncomfortable questions.

"So I was wondering could you get them together?" James finished. "If you could talk to the keeper?"

Big Jim stirred his coffee.

"I asked Karen," James said. "When I told her I was worried about the *elephants* not being together, she thought I was worried about *me!*"

Big Jim didn't laugh. "It does sound like a you-and-me situation. Elephants on different sides of town, and they want to get together? If you don't mind being compared to an elephant."

"I love being compared to an elephant!" James said. Big Jim had gone all quiet. James sat down and leaned across the table. "So could you do it? Or you figure out what to do, and *I* could do it?"

"I don't know anything about elephants," Big Jim said. "Elephants scare me, even that baby. Why don't *you* ask the keeper?"

"I did. She didn't care. Maybe if you. . . . You could tell the zoo to buy the baby!"

"No way they would listen to me. They probably have all kinds of 'no' reasons I can't even think of. Elephants cost big money. I'll think about it, but I don't see a way."

They rode back on the Metro, so quiet for so long, James said suddenly, "Hey! You missed your stop!"

"I'll ride you to your station," Big Jim said.

As the train slowed down at his stop, James didn't

want to leave Big Jim. "You want to come see Daisy? I can walk to my apartment from there."

The sun was already down behind the zoo's tall trees, but the air was still warm. James and Big Jim were the only people by the rail of the elephant yard. No keepers were out. Daisy stood by the building, slowly rubbing a stringy red rag under her eye. She didn't notice James.

Big Jim watched Menika and Beverly eating hay. "That's one smart elephant!" He pointed. Beverly pulled a tight packet of hay from a bale and tossed it up behind her. It hit her back, then tumbled to the ground in a loose pile. "She did that a minute ago, too. That's how she breaks it up so she can eat it."

"There's Daisy." James pointed. "That's the big sister."

Big Jim looked back and forth from Daisy to the others. "How can you tell that one's her sister?"

"Well, she's African like the baby, and the other two are Asian. See how her ears are bigger? I can't really tell it's her sister. I just know." James watched Big Jim, wanting him to care. He tried to remember something the circus woman had almost told him, something else about the baby, maybe about her family.

He sensed Daisy rumbling, and turned. She was striding toward them. Big Jim stepped back fast. "Whoaaa, there!"

"She's all right. Don't worry."

Daisy dropped the scrap of sock between her front feet and strained her trunk toward James. Then she turned it toward Big Jim. He took another step away.

James laughed. "She's just smelling. She wants to know about you. I think she knows you're my friend."

Stiffly, Big Jim stepped forward, and he held out his hand for Daisy to smell. She aimed her trunk at his boots.

"Watch," James said. "Daisy!" Her trunk came toward him. He breathed out a stream of air from deep inside, and Daisy sucked in the smells. "Apple pie, fries. She loves the news about food."

Big Jim laughed. "James, you are something else!"

"I do good research!" Then James was serious: "That's how I know elephants need their families. Mostly they stay with their families their whole life, going around together, helping each other. Like if one gets stuck in the mud at a watering hole they all pull him out. That's why Daisy keeps that red sock."

"That's a sock?"

"That was *my* sock. Remember I told you I got her sister's smell on it? Daisy loves it. She wants to be with her sister, Big Jim, and that circus is leaving tomorrow."

Big Jim was nodding, and James was hopeful, until Big Jim changed to shaking his head. He said, not really asking, "How am I going to get two elephants together? I'm a city boy, James. I don't know animals."

Daisy had picked up the red rag of a sock again, and she held it out toward James.

He leaned over the fence and said sharply, "I know, Daisy! I *know*!"

She swirled away from him, striding to the back of the yard, bumping by the hanging tire, kicking at the base of a barkless, branchless tree.

"Ooooh, boy!" Big Jim looked after her. "I should go. This job's getting me up early. You want me to walk you back?"

James watched Suzy and another keeper come out and begin to rake up old hay, one using the rake, the other holding a big shovel like a dustpan and dumping the hay into a wagon. Suzy kept looking at Daisy, watching, James was sure, in case Daisy did something crazy.

He pointed. "That's the keeper I tried to tell. She kept asking me about being a foster kid. *Please* talk to her."

Big Jim shrugged. "Why would she listen to me tell her to go buy an elephant? I'm sorry, boy. You want me to walk you back?"

"No. I can get there easy. See those lights?"

Big Jim looked until he was sure of the building where James lived now. "'Bye, then. I'll see you soon, James, now I know your number, now I know where you are."

After James watched Big Jim walk away, he kicked the ground like an elephant making dust. When he looked up, Suzy had come to the fence. Behind her, long shadows lay across the hard-packed dirt of the elephant yard.

"Who was that?" she asked, nosy again. "Your foster father?"

"He's my old dad," James said. "The one I told you about. My former foster father."

"The one you like?"

"Yeah."

"It's nice he came around."

"Can I ask you something?" James said.

"Sure." Suzy turned half away from him, probably to watch Daisy, but Daisy was already on her way over. She moved right in beside Suzy, looking at James. She put her sock down and stepped on it. She lifted the tip of her trunk between James and Suzy, curving it upward like a cup as if to catch their words, as if to be part of their conversation.

James loved Daisy so much, that minute, he felt halfway between laughing and crying, and either one would bust him wide open. Suzy looked as if she felt the same.

"Remember you said elephants like their families so much?" he asked. Suzy nodded. "Well, suppose you found out some other zoo or someplace had the sister or something for one of your elephants. Would you try to get her? So they could be together?"

Suzy didn't think long. "The sad thing is, I don't think so. It's complicated, getting an elephant. We need to know where our animals come from—their health and their history. We're part of an elephant breeding program, so we follow specific guidelines.

The zoo director and the animal managers plan years ahead for every new animal."

"But . . . guidelines!" James hated that word. "Don't you want families?"

"We're trying to save endangered animals, here and in the wild." Suzy patted Daisy's cheek. "We got Daisy just a few months ago. It won't be our turn to hit the budget again for a long time." She gave him a wave and started away. "Sometimes things can't happen the way you would wish."

No, James thought as he climbed the hill, things aren't happening right. Nobody would help—not Suzy, not Karen, not Big Jim—and they all had reasons. Maybe that man in the suit he'd seen outside the elephant yard the other day was the zoo director. James wished he'd told *him* about this!

"Daisy!" he shouted, though she was far behind him now. He remembered how strong, how fierce she had been, to find that baby, and the memory seemed to give him power. "*I'll* do it," he said loudly. "Myself!"

DOING WHAT TEACHER SAID

When James opened the door of the apartment, Martha's and Bill's eyes snapped away from the TV, right to him.

"We were worried about you!" Martha said. "We were going to call the police." James said nothing. Neither did Bill, though Bill looked up to stare at him between bites of his supper.

"You must come back on time. You should have phoned if you'd be late coming home." Martha wasn't calling James "sugar," now.

Why *hadn't* he phoned? He always liked it when somebody cared about him coming back. But he had forgotten Martha and Bill. All the afternoon with Big Jim, he had felt he *was* home.

He was grounded for a week, Martha said. He must go to school tomorrow and every day and come straight back and not go anywhere without permission. If they couldn't trust him, how could they be responsible for him? They had been told he was a good boy. If he wasn't, he couldn't stay here.

James thought Martha was right to say what she said, but as he got ready for bed he went on with his plans. If he was lucky, she would never learn what happened. He dressed carefully, putting on new jeans and the darkest of his new shirts. If he ended up in jail, at least Martha could be proud of the way he looked.

He wanted to start early, so as he lay in bed he made himself stay awake by saying over and over the names of all the kids in all the classes he'd ever been in. When he heard the TV go off, he looked at the clock. Exactly three quarters of an hour later, he threw back the covers and put on his sneakers.

He didn't go out the window. The window was too high for him without an elephant to help. From the tool drawer in the kitchen he took the hammer, a file, and a screwdriver. Then he went quietly out the door.

He used Daisy's tricks to move safely through the night streets, walking swiftly, standing in shadow when he sensed danger. He slipped into the zoo park through an opening between two fence posts. By bush and shadow he worked his way to the elephant yard. If there was a guard, he didn't seem to come around here.

The elephants were sleeping outside in the warm night, lying in great gray mounds. When they heard him, they heaved themselves up as if they were growing right out of the earth and came over to see him, all three. Menika and Beverly soon left, but as James began to work at the new lock on the outside gate, Daisy reached toward him. Luckily her trunk wasn't quite long enough to bother him.

The metal was thick and hard, and James's hands became sore. Checking over his shoulder for a guard but still trying to hurry, he pushed the file too hard and cut his knuckles. It took a long time to get the lock off—and then he was only half done.

When he moved across the little bridge to start on the inside lock, Daisy became frisky as a puppy—a great, towering giant of a puppy. She ran her trunk over his hands, over his tools. When he brushed her away, she ran off snorting, flipping her trunk around, then came hurrying back to bother him some more.

When he finally had the second lock off, he swung the gates open, and Daisy ran out. He had to call to her to wait. When he'd closed the gates, she helped him up, and they were off.

Daisy went down into the creek and turned north. No need for James to tell her which way to go tonight! When they moved out onto the streets near the mall, though, he twice had to remind her to freeze when cars were coming.

As they entered the mall parking lot, he felt vibrations in her neck and face. He was sure the owner slept nearby, so he patted her, hard. "Daisy! Shhh!" She seemed to understand. Though she was tense, ears out, trunk high, she made no noise.

The circus tent was folded, the ticket office lay flat, the ring sections were stacked, all ready to load for a quick getaway in the morning. The sides of the trucks were down, and Hanzvadzi's window was closed. As James slid to the ground, he heard her squealing, and thumping against her walls. Soon the monkeys were fussing in their truck.

"Daisy!" James reached up to pat her face, trying to give her a feeling of calm. "Daisy! Shhh! Shhhh!" When she had lowered her trunk and stood quiet, he said, "Tell Hanzvadzi! Shhhh!" He stroked the side of the truck, slowly, slowly. "Shhh!" Daisy moved her ears and gave a low rumble. Hanzvadzi quieted.

James climbed behind the truck's cab and found the rope he'd seen the owner use to lower the side. He unwound it from its cleat and pulled. The side didn't budge.

Still holding the rope, he jumped to the ground, braced his feet, and tried again. A shimmer of movement told him just how heavy the side was. But James had brought along more power than he could possibly need.

"Daisy!" he whispered. She took the rope with her trunk and simply walked away. By the time the side of the truck was folded up, Hanzvadzi's trunk was reaching through the bars.

While Daisy kept the rope taut, James leapt back on the truck and tied it off. Then Daisy moved close, and the two trunks hugged and petted one another, weaving in and out, sliding up and down. But though James felt a low rumbling, the elephants didn't squeal.

He tapped one of the vertical bars on the side of the truck with his hammer. It was strong enough to hold a baby elephant, he thought, but not nearly as strong as the cages in the elephant house. "Daisy!" He curved his hand and arm around a bar as a trunk would and pretended to pull.

She popped the first bar out easily and flung it behind her. In five minutes, bars were scattered like bent Pick-Up Sticks across the grass, and there was a wide opening in the side of the cage. Hanzvadzi stood two feet above the ground, picking up a leg and putting it down again. She seemed afraid to jump.

The boards of the folded-up ticket office, James thought, should be strong enough to hold her. "Daisy!"

Daisy put her tusks beneath the boards and, with her trunk securing them like a bungee cord across the top, carried them to the truck. With James guiding, she placed them at the truck opening as a ramp. A few seconds later, Hanzvadzi was on the ground beside her.

Then the real elephant reunion began. Hanzvadzi and Daisy made all the joyful squeals and trumpeting, all the ear slapping and rumblings, they had been holding in since James said, "Shhh!" They ran around and around each other, their faces throbbing, wet and shining. They wrapped trunks together and hugged so hard Hanzvadzi's front feet lifted from the ground.

"Happy New Year!" came a loud shout. The feeling fit the occasion, but it certainly wasn't an elephant talking. James looked behind him, ready to run. But when the same voice began repeating, "Turn left! Turn left!" he knew it was only a parrot. The other animals were barking, neighing, chattering, thumping, louder and louder.

James felt like trumpeting, himself, but he wanted to leave while they were still safe. He stepped close and shouted to Daisy. She ignored him, and he had to back away from the stomping feet and storm of noise. Daisy stopped hugging Hanzvadzi, spun around, and began picking up cage bars and tossing them high. James backed farther away.

Then James heard a sharp crack. In a single instant both elephants went silent. Like a bad dream returning, the circus man came around the front end of the truck. His fist hit the hood, then he bent down, checking the tires.

In a flurry of motion, the elephants bolted, Hanzvadzi running alongside Daisy, bumping into her legs. The man looked up with a jerk and stared after them. He stared at his open, empty cage and the mangled bars all over the ground. His face was full of confusion and rage. He gave the truck a terrific whack.

James had never been so close to anyone so angry. He raced after the fleeing elephants, screaming, "Daisy!"

"What the. . . . Hey! Hey, *you*!" This time, for sure, the owner knew that James was there.

James stopped running so he could shout, "Daisy!"

with every bit of his strength. He heard the owner's voice, cursing and shouting for help. He heard the owner's footsteps coming fast. As James ran again, the parrot's call behind him, "Slow down, you fool!" wasn't funny at all.

Though he managed to stay ahead of the man, James was falling farther behind Daisy. He stopped and screamed to her, lifting his voice from the bottom of his lungs, "Daisy! Stop!"

He looked over his shoulder to see where the circus owner was now. Though he was closer to James now, he was stumbling backward so quickly he almost fell.

James turned the other way and saw Daisy rushing toward him, Hanzvadzi beside her. With each step, she seemed larger and more powerful. Her trumpet blasted every other sound from the air. For a moment it seemed to blast away the air itself. A few days ago, James would have been terrified. Tonight, he had no doubt this huge and raging elephant was coming to rescue him.

The owner *was* terrified. He raced away from the two-elephant stampede even faster than he had run after James. On the far side of his empty truck, he leaned over, pounding uselessly on the hood.

Daisy didn't stop as she scooped James up, nor did she help him climb onto her back. She simply curved her trunk under his bottom and kept running. James rode as if he was in a swing, hugging Daisy's upper trunk as she and Hanzvadzi raced across the parking lot, away.

The owner was chasing them again, shouting, "Stop!" As they came to the avenue, he called, "Police!" and "Taxi!" He soon must have realized that calling "Taxi!" on a deserted road in the early morning dark made as much sense as commanding fleeing elephants to halt. He stopped running, and James could barely hear his last words: "I'll find you! There's not many places an elephant can go! I'll find you!"

Daisy ran silently on, and soon they were safely in the woods. James looked back at Hanzvadzi, trudging behind with weary steps now, her trunk holding onto Daisy's tail. Living in that cage, she wasn't used to so much exercise.

When they came to the creek, Daisy finally stopped. She helped James onto her back, then sprayed some water on Hanzvadzi. The next time she swung her trunk up, great, cold, plopping drops landed on James! Why did elephants think this was such a treat? Did Daisy think she was doing him a favor? Cooling him off? Washing him? Or was all this spraying for herself?

He heard a soft gurgle, then her trunk whipped up on her other side, delivering another cold spray. Two sprays and he was soaked through! He beat his heels *rat-a-tat* onto her neck, laughing and calling, "Daisy! Stop! You like that, not me! Stop that, you crazy elephant!"

Perhaps she understood, for the next time she filled her trunk, she put the tip into her mouth and tilted her head back. James heard the water pouring down inside her. The water had cheered them up, though. Hanzvadzi was playing like a baby in a bath, splashing with her trunk, drinking and spraying. When they started again, the elephants walked slowly.

James was exhausted. He longed for his bed, though he knew Martha would make him get up and go to school, no matter how tired he was. School! It seemed so long since he'd been in Ms. Jackson's room. Monday! The research notes were due in a few hours. He'd learned a lot about elephants in one week, but little was written down, and he wouldn't dare to write the rest.

Was it just last week his class had visited the zoo and Ms. Jackson said, "James, why don't you take an elephant?" What would she think if she could see him now, taking not one elephant but two! If they catch me, James thought, I'll just say I'm doing what my teacher said. He laughed out loud, and a moment later he was sound asleep, his head on his hands on top of Daisy's rough and hairy head.

When he woke, they were back in the elephant yard. He climbed down wearily, Daisy's trunk helping him all the way. Hanzvadzi stood close, her trunk around Daisy's leg, as Menika, then Beverly, came to smell and touch her, snort and back away, then come close to smell and touch her again.

James wanted Hanzvadzi to know she had another friend. He leaned over and slowly breathed out toward her. Whatever his breath smelled of now, she seemed to enjoy it.

Daisy rumbled, and a moment later James heard a garbage truck go by. He left, closing both gates behind him. There was no way he could fix the locks. As he ran by their cage, the gibbons were beginning their morning howl.

He climbed into bed still tingling with the excitement of what he and Daisy had done. But as he watched the morning light increase outside his window, as he watched his clock move toward getting-up time, James grew lonely and scared. He had no doubt the circus owners would soon be at the zoo.

A LITTLE CONVERSATION

At breakfast, Martha repeated her severe message: James was to go to school and come right back. He was to go nowhere without permission.

James nodded. He was watching a news report about the little elephant that had suddenly appeared at the National Zoo. Live coverage from the elephant yard showed only Hanzvadzi's legs. She was hiding behind Daisy, who was looking fierce.

"Keepers were astonished," the announcer said, "when they found they had four elephants instead of three." When Bill hurried away, he left the television on, but there wasn't any news for James: "No one knows how it got here. Keepers don't even know if this baby is male or female!"

The instant Martha left, James dialed Big Jim's number. Mama answered. She told him Big Jim had gone. "He tore out of here this morning. Didn't touch his nice breakfast. Left the radio on. Didn't even say good-bye!"

James barely said good-bye, himself, before he

hung up. As he ran to the zoo, he knew that this time for sure Martha would find out he had disobeyed her. He didn't care.

A large crowd was watching the elephant yard, with more people coming all the time. The circus man and woman were standing at the fence, talking to Suzy and other keepers, and to the zoo director.

Only Daisy and Hanzvadzi were in the yard, their backs to the stone building, Hanzvadzi tight by Daisy's side. If Daisy moved a step, Hanzvadzi moved, too. Every few minutes, Daisy's trunk swung around to lie gently along Hanzvadzi's back or gently touched her ear.

Nothing else about Daisy was gentle. She looked dangerous, even to James. She shook her head, cracking her ears against her shoulders. Her legs and trunk swung restlessly. Clearly, she would fight anyone who tried to take Hanzvadzi away.

James wanted to know what the zoo people and the circus people were saying, but he couldn't let them see him. Bending his knees, he worked his way through the crowd of long legs and small children. Soon he could hear the outraged voice of the circus owner, then the voice of the baffled zoo director: "But we have no idea how . . . !"

"I saw them!" the circus man said. "Both elephants running, and riding on that big one was a kid who's been hanging around. I'm sure it was the same kid."

"Daisy's been acting strange all week," a keeper

said. "Almost like she smelled something in the wind."

"Someone's been planning this," the circus woman said. "That kid was out a few days ago, asking all kinds of questions about Pumpkin."

Suzy winced. *"Pumpkin?!"*

"Our elephant. We got her on Halloween. If you find that kid, you'll know who took her."

"There are hundreds of kids here every day," the other keeper said impatiently, but Suzy turned and looked over the crowd. James ducked behind two people holding out tape recorders.

"It had to be someone from here," the circus man said.

"None of us has tried riding Daisy yet," Suzy told the director.

"Whoever did it," the circus woman said, "we need Pumpkin now! We have a show in Cincinnati, Wednesday. We've got to leave."

"We can't get her out," Suzy said. "Daisy won't let us near her. We don't want them any more upset than they are now."

"Shoot them with a tranquilizer!" the circus man suggested.

"We never tranquilize an elephant," the director said, "unless it's very serious."

"This *is* serious, believe me," the man said. "You may have a lawsuit on your hands."

"We're going to give them something to eat," the director said, "and a chance to calm down. We'll give them half an hour and see what happens. Meanwhile, let's see what else we can find out. We need more information before we decide what to do."

People began talking in separate conversations, murmuring urgently. A man with a microphone moved in close. James felt a hand on his shoulder. He spun around, ready to run.

"James!" Karen's voice seemed as loud as a shout. "I heard about that elephant. Is it . . . ?"

Making frantic shushing signs, James took her hand to lead her away. He'd taken only a few steps when another, heavier hand fell on him. Again, he was certain he'd been caught.

"James! You all right? Soon as I heard the news, I knew. . . ."

"Hello, Mr. Big Jim," Karen said.

James saw Big Jim look up, saw the flicker of worry on his face change to a smile. "Hey, Ms. Karen! You here for my boy?"

"I knew he . . . cared about these elephants. I was afraid he'd skip school."

"That's why I came," Big Jim said smoothly. "I heard he's been skipping school. He's got to stop it!"

James grinned. "Noooo! You both came to see if it was me that . . ." His heart was singing. The last time he'd seen Big Jim and Karen together was the day she took James away. Now they had each come to be sure he was all right, maybe to help him. He pulled them out of the crowd, a little way up the hill. But when he turned and saw his other friends, the elephants, huddled and scared, his heart stopped singing.

Karen was shaking Big Jim's hand. "So. How you doing?"

"About half," Big Jim said. "You?"

"Fine," Karen said. "Just fine, thanks."

Then: Nothing happened. Karen, James, and Big Jim stood in a row and watched the elephants.

Daisy's body tensed as if she heard a noise that threatened danger. A minute later, the steel door slid open, just a foot. Two keepers looked out.

Daisy took a step forward. Her ears were out, her tail was up, her trunk was high. A front leg pushed Hanzvadzi behind her, then kicked the ground.

"Steady, babe!" Big Jim stepped back. "James, you sure that's your friend?"

James took Big Jim's hand again. "It's okay. She has to. She's guarding her little sister."

While one keeper kept an eye on Daisy, the other took two steps into the yard, carrying plastic buckets.

Daisy roared a warning and flipped out her trunk.

The keeper dropped the buckets, spilling their fruit. She hurried back inside, and the steel door closed. As the echo of Daisy's roar faded, the crowd was completely silent. She had stopped even the circus people's talk.

Hanzvadzi's trunk skittered up along Daisy's side, reached under Daisy's belly. Daisy flung her trunk across Hanzvadzi's shoulder and stood glaring at the fruit.

Only her anger, James saw, was preventing them all from acting immediately. "They're not even talking about keeping her here," he told Big Jim and Karen. "Nobody down there even knows they are sisters!"

Neither Big Jim nor Karen answered him.

Daisy and Hanzvadzi walked over by the steel door. Hanzvadzi's trunk poked at the scattered fruit. She picked out an apple and curled it up into her mouth.

"She's darling," Karen said softly.

"Why wouldn't the zoo just pay them and let her stay?" Big Jim asked James.

"The keeper said they're careful how they get new animals," James told him. "They have guidelines. Like Karen."

"Our guidelines are to protect children, James," Karen said, a little sharply. Then she smiled. "I don't know anything about elephants except what you've told me. But even I can see those two belong together."

James nodded. "They're sisters." He could sense Karen and Big Jim each thinking that he couldn't possibly know that. He couldn't explain how he knew, but he was absolutely sure.

Still: Nothing happened. Big Jim didn't seem to even be thinking about the problem. He smiled and nodded as Daisy stepped lightly on a melon, squashing it before she put it in her mouth. He watched her quickly toss in an apple, a pear, some oranges. "She's making fruit salad in there!" He laughed, but then he asked, "So! How are we going to get these zoo people to keep that baby?"

In the flatness of Big Jim's voice, James heard a familiar mischief. He flushed with relief, then hope, as Big Jim went on: "How do we help them to forget these guidelines and look at what's good for the animals?"

James wished Karen would answer, but she was absorbed in watching the elephants. More and more people were pressing around Suzy and the others, people with microphones, people with children on their shoulders. James could hear the impatient voices.

He grew impatient himself, with Big Jim's slow talking. It would be hard to find Hanzvadzi once she was in Cincinnati or someplace. If she was taken away, Daisy might go crazy with sadness or rage. She might not trust even James anymore. He gave Big Jim's foot a kick.

Big Jim didn't even glance at him, but turned to Karen. "You believe elephants are social animals?"

"Look!" She pointed. "And that's what James's report says. Right?"

"Right!" James shouted it out, glad to have a part at last.

"Then why don't the zoo people do what they should for these social animals?" Big Jim asked. "Might be they could use a little social work."

Karen giggled. "For elephants?"

Big Jim went on: "Ms. Karen, would you have a little conversation with James's keeper friend, if he can get her up here?"

Karen looked puzzled. "If you think it might do some good. . . ."

James was off running before she finished.

People stood five deep along the fence now, watching two elephants eat fruit. The television news, Daisy's fierce trumpet, the mystery of the baby elephant, the huddle of people deciding what to do, had all created an irresistible excitement. James passed a kid pulling on a pant leg. "Mommy! Let's go!" Mommy didn't budge.

Staying out of the circus people's line of sight the way he'd learned to stay downwind of an elephant, James worked his way to Suzy. She leaned on the rail, her chin on her hand, staring at Daisy and Hanzvadzi as if she was trying to figure out a puzzle. He crouched and tapped her arm.

She looked surprised to see him, and when James motioned her to be silent and to come away, she looked annoyed. "Please?" he whispered. "Not far. Just for a minute."

She nodded. He led her through the crowd, hoping she'd let him explain before she got mad.

"*I* need to talk to *you*," she said as soon as it was safe. "The gates are open again. Somebody cut the locks."

"I know," James said.

"I had to tell the director. I didn't tell the circus people. I don't know what you think you're doing, if you are doing something. You or someone. You can't

119

fool around with wild animals. Elephants can be dangerous. What's going on?"

"If I tell you something, will you do something?" he asked. "I mean, if I tell you everything I know, will you talk with someone for a few minutes before you tell the others?"

She looked at him doubtfully.

"I know how the baby got here," he said. "I was there."

Suzy gave a sharp, angry sigh—almost an elephant *whoosh*, James thought. She checked the elephant yard. Half the fruit was left. "All right."

Quickly James told her the story, more than he'd told Karen or Big Jim. He even told her that he was the one who'd cut the locks. He hoped that even if Suzy was angry, *she* could believe how hard Daisy had searched, *she* would understand how much Daisy needed Hanzvadzi.

At first, Suzy seemed not to believe him. Then, as James described the elephants' reunions: the first one, when they could only touch trunks through a window, and the second, when they danced together at last, she didn't look angry, she simply looked stunned.

He finished, "I'm sure the baby is Daisy's sister. The circus got her just a few months ago. She's from Zimbabwe, too."

Suzy stared into the yard. "That's so unlikely."

"So, now? Come talk to my social worker? She knows a lot about families."

"Your social worker!"

"Please? You said you would. She's my friend, too."

As they walked, because Suzy seemed to care, James told her: "My foster father's here, too. Big Jim, my former foster father I told you about. He came again."

After everyone was introduced, nobody said anything for much too long. James watched Suzy looking Karen over, looking at the strap of Karen's sack pulling at her long, soft dress with the pink and brown flowers.

Karen was staring at Suzy, too. For once in her life, James thought, Karen doesn't know what to say! He wished Big Jim would start the talk.

When Suzy's eyes shifted back to the elephant yard, James said quickly, "See, Daisy and . . ."

Big Jim broke in: "We were thinking, Suzy, maybe Karen could . . ."

Finally, Karen started, using the careful voice she used when she asked James questions, guiding him to make a good choice: "*You* know elephants. Does it seem to *you* those two need each other? Do *you* think it's possible they're sisters? Isn't there a way the zoo could help them stay together—no matter what the rules . . . ?"

Suzy didn't like that, at *all*. She burst in on Karen's calm: "Couldn't I say the same to you? Can *you* make everything come out right every time? For every family?" She flicked her ankus back and forth from

James to Big Jim, back and forth, back and forth. "The way it *should* be? It's not so simple!"

Karen didn't like *that* at all. Her voice came quick and shrill: "Wait a minute! We're talking about elephants . . . !"

James was amazed—he was ashamed!—that Suzy would say that. He looked away from her, away from Big Jim, away from Karen.

Then Suzy was talking to him. "I don't know what you wanted to happen here, James, but I should get back. I'm sorry. Good luck." She sounded disgusted, but she gave him half a smile before she walked away.

"It didn't work!" James told Big Jim. "Nothing happened! That was stupid!"

Big Jim pressed James's shoulder. He motioned him to talk more softly and pointed toward Karen. But she was a few steps away now, standing by herself, staring at the elephants. She didn't seem to hear.

"She tried," Big Jim went on softly. "And we don't know yet. Maybe something did happen. It's not over. If Suzy's mad, it means she's thinking. You'd best go help her."

FIERCE AS DAISY

Daisy and Hanzvadzi were still close together, still tense, when James crouched beside Suzy at the rail.

The zoo director was telling her, "Of course it would be nice to have a baby, but we're not an animal shelter. We can't make that big a change in plans so quickly. We need to know more about her, her health, where she came from, all that. We have to know where the animal fits into the long-term program."

"Her health?!" The circus man broke in. "My animals pass inspection every time! I can show you papers on this animal. We work with very good zoos, a very good animal supplier. . . ."

When he mentioned where he'd bought Hanzvadzi, Suzy gasped. "That's the place that sold Daisy to the farm where we got her!"

A memory tickled James's mind: The circus woman had almost told him something else, that first day, something else about Hanzvadzi and her . . . He touched Suzy's arm and whispered, "Ask her what their supplier said about Pumpkin's family."

When Suzy asked, the circus woman answered, "He said Pumpkin and her sister were orphans."

"How could he know they were sisters?" the circus man snapped at her.

"He *called* them sisters," the woman snapped back. "You heard him. He knew they'd been captured from the same herd. With elephants, a herd *is* family. And he *knew* they were orphans because all the adult elephants were shot."

"What did he say about her sister?" the zoo director asked. "Where's her sister now?"

"He didn't say. I guess he sold her to someone else."

"This is what we've been wanting!" Suzy spoke almost angrily, and only to the zoo director now. "To have related elephants living together, like in the wild! If we're serious about building a family herd, we should jump at this chance."

"Extraordinary." The director stared at the elephants. The fruit was gone, and Hanzvadzi was smelling one of the plastic buckets, touching her trunk tip to it here and there, like a doctor examining a chest with a stethoscope. No one near the zoo director said a word.

Finally, he sighed. "Extraordinary. That they could find each other! Well, they must stay together. We'll buy her."

He spoke so softly, James didn't believe it was decided till he heard the buzz of talk and the cheers as the news rippled out through the crowd.

The circus woman jumped in quickly, a tiny smile on her face. "We paid a good price for that elephant, and all this publicity has made her even more valuable. She's worth a lot."

"No you don't!" Suzy said. "The publicity works the other way. You hike up her price so we can't afford her, and *no* one in the whole United States would go to your circus. They'd know you kept the elephant sisters apart."

"Enough!" The circus man looked at his watch. "It's ridiculous to spend more time on this. We have to leave. That animal needs a lot of training, and I've got better ways to spend my time. Give us a fair price, and you can have her."

The zoo director beamed. "Come to my office, and we'll talk. You'll be on your way to Cincinnati in half an hour."

When they were out of sight, James stood and stretched his aching legs. He grinned at Suzy. "Thank you!"

"Thank *you*! And, James? I hope you didn't mind what I said up there. That woman really burned me up, talking about buying an elephant as if it was so easy."

"Yeah. Well." He couldn't be mad at Suzy, now, for what she said about him and Big Jim. "But I've got to go." Big Jim and Karen would soon be hurrying away.

"Come back later when things settle down. I want to hear *all* of your story."

Even before James got close, he was waving and shouting, "Big Jim!" and Big Jim was shouting, "James!"

James ran and leapt up onto Big Jim's back, pounding his shoulders, the way he used to. "She can stay! She can stay! She can stay!" James hugged Big Jim back to front, and Big Jim's strong arms reached around to hug James front to back.

Then Big Jim spun around and around, the way *he* used to. "You did a *job*, James!" He spun around the other way once, twice, then stopped. "I'm getting old for this, and you are getting heavy."

When Big Jim put him down, James asked, "Do you want to meet Daisy? You should meet Daisy!"

"I got to go, James. This job. . . ."

"Come on. Just for a minute?"

"I met Daisy," Big Jim said firmly. "She smelled me, remember?"

"She'd love to smell you again!" James took Big Jim's hand. "Karen, too. Where's Karen?"

Karen Grande came slowly toward them, watching them both so hard James suddenly felt shy. "Congratulations, James. I don't quite understand what happened, but I think you did something wonderful here."

"Big Jim, too," James said. "And Suzy. Suzy got fierce as Daisy for keeping the baby here! You should have heard her. So you too, Karen. Thanks for talking to her."

Karen smiled and nodded, and once more everyone was quiet. It was time for someone to leave, James thought, but no one left.

Karen said, "So, Mr. Big Jim, you living with your aunt now?"

James felt Big Jim's arm sudden and heavy on his shoulder. He felt Big Jim's body next to his go perfectly still. "Yes. I just call her Mama. She raised me."

"Do you think I could meet your aunt? You think she'd let me visit her home? Is it a house or an apartment?"

"A house," Big Jim said softly. "A good house. Not fancy, but he could have his own room." He swallowed. "Mama would be pleased to meet you. Mama loves James."

"May I call her then, this afternoon? This evening? Does she have a job?"

Big Jim was so nervous he couldn't remember Mama's number right, so James said it. Big Jim was so nervous he couldn't write it down, so James wrote it.

"Call this evening," Big Jim said. "Do you think . . . ?"

"Let me visit your aunt, first. Then we'll talk." Karen shook Big Jim's hand, and James's hand, too, though she didn't usually do that.

James spoke up then, feeling fierce himself: "Martha might not even want me anymore, anyway. I'm skipping school right this minute."

"I've probably got three messages from her waiting at the office!" Karen's face grew stern, and she started to say something more, but Big Jim jumped in.

"What do you think, Ms. Karen? Let's us let this boy skip school, just one more time. He's been doing good work for these elephants, but he looks poorly—he needs his sleep. Let him stay home one more day. Then back he goes to school, bright-eyed and ready, every morning. Right, James?"

"Right!"

"All right, Ms. Karen?"

She looked from one to the other, and now she was letting her smile shine out. "All right. Good-bye, then." She hoisted up her bag and left.

After a minute Big Jim said, as if he was talking to himself, "Don't get too excited, James. There's lots in the way. Karen has to talk to her boss; maybe she'd have to ask the court about it. My home's not 'fit,' remember. And this place that's got you now *is* 'fit': home-cooked food, probably iron your shirts. I bet you take a bath every night. Don't interrupt me, James. I know all that doesn't 'fit' you like I do. But I certainly know how to tell you to take a bath!"

"I was *going* to say: Why don't you and me learn to cook?"

Big Jim looked shocked. He looked truly shocked at James's suggestion. He looked as if a remark had been made in such bad taste he had no words to answer. He patted James's shoulder and turned to watch Menika and Beverly walk into the yard and hurry over to Hanzvadzi.

Soon Big Jim said, "I got to go. I got to get to work.

I got to phone Mama and tell her not to offer Ms. Karen a thing to eat. You bring me to meet Daisy another day. Get some sleep! I've got an idea what you've been doing nights. I won't mention it again. It's over. Get some sleep, then get going on your famous report. There's a lot of us waiting to read it."

Much later, when the crowd was smaller, James walked over and stood by Suzy at the rail. She and another keeper were planning what to feed Hanzvadzi.

Daisy's trunk worked some hay up into a little bundle, used it to scratch her leg, then put it in her mouth. Hanzvadzi was facing her, standing close and rubbing her eye with the end of her trunk as if she was very, very sleepy. Watching her, James couldn't help but yawn.

When the other keeper left, he thanked Suzy again, and Suzy again thanked him. There was a happy murmur from the crowd, and they turned to look.

Hanzvadzi, her tail high over her rump, was running far from Daisy, chasing sparrows who'd been picking up bits of hay. When a few birds tried to land, she shook her ears at them. All the time, Daisy watched calmly, her trunk looped over one of her tusks now, resting.

"Do you think I could talk to Daisy?" James missed her badly. All this time he'd been at the rail, she hadn't noticed him.

"*You* can do just about anything you want," Suzy said. "But not out here. I don't want to give any other kids ideas—*your* kind of ideas. Daisy's a wild animal, remember. We're going to take them inside soon and close the house to give them some peace. Come around and meet me at the door."

After Suzy had led James behind the barrier which separated the public from the cages inside the elephant house, she stopped by the cage where the little elephant family now stood. "I need to know something. Do you like the name Pumpkin?"

"I hate it! I call her Hanzvadzi. It means sister in Zimbabwe. And brother. Also cousin. All the kids in the family. Whoever she is for Daisy, she's Daisy's *hanzvadzi*."

"Han-zvad-zi. Hanzvadzi. Perfect," Suzy said. "Perfect. But, then, you know . . . ?"

"I know. Daisy's a silly name, too, for an elephant."

"Yes."

"But. . . ." James shrugged. "We can't make *everything* come out right. Daisy's Daisy! She knows the name."

Daisy's ears swung out. James watched her trunk rise into the S salute and turn in his direction. He watched her stride toward him, waggling her ears. Hanzvadzi came with her, and James heard the slow, comfortable sound of rough skins scraping as two elephants walked close together, side by side.

AUTHOR'S NOTE

Could an elephant really do the extraordinary things Daisy does in *Nightwalkers*? After reading widely about elephant history, biology, and behavior, after observing the elephants who live at the National Zoological Park in Washington, D.C., and talking with the people who care for them, I believe an elephant could.

Ever since people have known elephants, it seems, they have reported amazing stories about them. Scientists working in the wild have observed the intensity and complexity of elephants' family lives and often speak of profound similarities between elephant and human families. Whatever is unlikely in Daisy's story, I believe, comes from gathering so many incidents into one animal's life. Her actions are exceptional, but they are within the bounds of possible elephant behavior.

The zoo scenes here are based on the progressive program at the National Zoo, with its single herd of Asian and African elephants. I'm grateful to the skilled keepers, particularly Marie Galloway and Debbie Flynn, for their help. John Lehnhardt, the zoo's assistant curator for mammals and an advocate for elephants worldwide, was also generous with his time and attention. His careful, forthright answers, and stories from his own experience gave me a richer understanding of elephants and helped me grasp the range and limits of their behavior.

John Lehnhardt and his staff grace their work with confidence, firm practicality, great good humor, a willingness to learn from the elephants—and to teach humans. They share their knowledge freely with any visitor, believing only educated changes in human behavior will save the threatened existence of Earth's elephants. Of course, the zoo staff is not responsible for any errors in what is, after all, a work of fiction.

The National Zoo is part of the Smithsonian Institution, partly supported by federal taxes, free to all, and a wonderful place to visit. If you go, however, don't expect to find Daisy, Hanzvadzi, Beverly, or Menika there. The elephants in this book, like the humans, are fictional characters. You may notice that I have taken some minor liberties in describing the elephant yard and elephant-care routines.

Wildlife policy in the many African nations where elephants live changes frequently. In 1995, for instance, Zimbabwe suspended the culling of elephant herds for at least a year.

I'm grateful to Madelyn Andrews and her colleagues at the D. C. Commission on Social Services for explaining the policies and practices of Washington's foster care system. My family and many friends also helped in the telling of this story. Rather than list them all, I will simply thank two.

My oldest friend, Gretchen Sue Langrock Viederman, grew up to be a social worker who helps children who have no family with whom to live. At just the right moment in a friendship of many years, Gretchen traveled halfway around the world, rode an elephant, and reported back to me about that as well.

Jenny Hawkins, a small dog, taught me that I live in a sea of smells and sounds about which I know almost nothing.